LUKEWARM LIES

DISCOVERING HALF TRUTHS OF THE 21ST CENTURY CHURCH

C.J. KUENZLI

Unless otherwise identified, all Scripture quotations have been taken from the
NEW AMERICAN STANDARD BIBLE®, Copyright © 1960,1962,1963,19
68,1971,1972,1973,1975,1977,1995 by The Lockman Foundation.

Scripture quotations mark NIV are taken from *The Holy Bible, New International
Version*®, NIV®. Copyright © 1973, 1978, 1984, 2011 by Biblica, Inc.™

Scripture quotations mark TPT are taken from *The Passion Translation*®.
Copyright © 2017 by Passion & Fire Ministries, Inc.

Published by

BURKHART BOOKS ⚓

Bedford , Texas
www.BurkhartBooks.com

Dedication

To:

PAPA

A, B, & Z

Acknowledgments

This book was downloaded into my heart during a sweet time of worship, conversation, and prayer with the Lord. Its contents are birthed out of the journey He's taken me on these last ten years. I am grateful for the opportunity to share what He's given me.

Bethany Kuenzli! My wife! My rib! My heart! Ever since we've met, you have had a "yes" in your heart for what God was doing in us, around us and through us. You are the most beautiful expression of God's love for me. Thank you for championing me when I fall down, for seeing me when my eyes are clouded and for hearing me when I feel I've lost my voice. I owe so much of who I've become to you! I daily thank God that we collided; for I have never been the same since, and I am far better for it.

I am forever indebted to my parents, Peter and Jana Kuenzli! You both stewarded a culture of love, creativity, and expression that set me up for exploring the unseen. I like to think that my time with LEGO's, dad reading me stories and all of my "themed" papers (punishments) primed the pump for my creative writing.

Marcus Bellamy, my pastor, and friend! Wisdom and favor follow you like a sweet aroma, for you have set yourself before the King of kings; which gives you access to lead and impact nations. Thank you for your counsel, blessings and (most of all) friendship.

Bill and Mary Buckley! You two have stirred my heart in a way I can't explain. Thank you for calling out the gold in me and reminding me who I am in the Father's eyes. You have championed the Kingdom so well, and this book is evidence of your impact in my life.

Thanks to Russell and Summer Mord! You two have been a harbor in the tempest. Russell, you have not only challenged me to chase after God harder, but you've shown me that it comes from resting in Him. You two are such a sweet example of Christian leadership and are bringing life back to that title.

To my Mississippi parents, Darin and Janet Beall! Through thick and thin, you have been there for my family and me. You ask the hard questions, but you laugh and love even harder. Thank you for your love, acceptance, and approval!

Finally, Tim Boden, thank you! I get to sit before a spiritual savant, who creatively and uniquely oozes the essence of the Kingdom with every intentional word. You've allowed me to be my imperfect self, cultivate my creative side, and freed me to chase after God! You once said, "if you have a book in you … WRITE IT!" Thank you for the nudge!

Contents

Foreword

Caleb Kuenzli's book Lukewarm Lies reads just like he lives—spontaneous, creative, and passionate! To me, a great read is one in which you can hear the author's voice. In this book, I hear Caleb's voice for truth and God the Father calling us to His heart. We all have some religion in us, and we usually need help seeing it. Caleb's book puts the light on half-truths so we can see the whole truth. I hope you will read it with the attitude in which it was written, with an open heart and an open mind!

Bill Buckley
Mississippi State Director,
Fellowship Of Christian Athletes
Board Chairman,
Land of the Living

Preface

Let's take a look at Revelation 3:14-16 (NASB):

"To the angel of the church in Laodicea write: The Amen, the faithful and true Witness, the Beginning of the creation of God, says this: 'I know your deeds, that you are neither cold nor hot; I wish that you were cold or hot. So because you are lukewarm and neither hot nor cold, I will spit you out of My mouth."

For years this passage has been taught as, "it is far better that you be on fire for the gospel or frozen for hell, instead of lukewarm with one foot in glory and the other in damnation!" What? Why? Jesus says, I prefer that you are hot or cold! Only those that are lukewarm will be spewed from His mouth!

But what's wrong with cold? Why has "cold" gotten such a bad rap? Cold water is refreshing! It's like a sweet kiss of life on a parched mouth. Imagine drinking bottled water straight from the mountain of God! Ahh, my soul is revived!

What about hot water? Hot water is for healing. Imagine having spent the entire day hiking out in God's creation and returning home for a hot shower. It's like a soothing balm rolling over your aching muscles and soul; as if being massaged by the very hand of God.

It's said that the Laodiceans made aqueducts to funnel the springs and rivers to town, but by the time the water arrived it was … lukewarm! The cold water had warmed up, and the hot springs cooled along its journey. Refreshing was lost. Healing properties were gone. It was now filled with bacteria that would make the people sick. So when Jesus said they were lukewarm, they knew exactly what He was talking about.

It's possible that Christ was saying, "I wish you had purpose! I wish you were refreshing for others or healing for others! But since you have lost your potency, you have no part with Me!"

The issue with the 21st Century church is we've moved away from the mountain of God (the cool waters) and away from the healing springs of God (the hot waters) and settled for a version of truth that is easy to swallow and even easier to digest!

This is why we have a lazy "body" that's constantly "sick." We've been drinking parasite infested water served up on a platter by the enemy of our souls. He delights in the fact that we only read certain verses from Scripture so that it emphasizes a half-truth!

I know there are a few sections of the Bible that are a bit too cold, while others are a tad too hot; they happen to sting my teeth and tongue when I sip on ithem But it may be time we take the hot oil of the Spirit of God and allow Him to heal the aching places within. And it's probably time we take the cold, refreshing, passages of God's reviving nature in the Word and allow it to shock our systems back into the battle that's waging around us!

A lukewarm church is full of lazy Christians. A vibrant and alive body of Christ will not only read good Bible stories but live the Kingdom in each and every moment!

Introduction

The offense that's slipping its way in and out of the church today is a result of a half-truth Gospel. Throughout this book, I hope that you can discover the truths of the Bible in order to pick up the fullness of God; for yourself, the church, and the world.

Truth | noun - the quality or state of being true
- that which is true or in accordance with fact or reality
- a fact or belief that is accepted as true

True | adj
- in accordance with fact or reality
- accurate or exact
- loyal or faithful 4) honest

True | adv
- truly
- accurately or without variation

True | verb - bring (an object, wheel, or other construction) into the exact shape, alignment, or position required

Untruth | noun - a lie or false statement (often used euphemistically) a) the quality of being false

Lie | noun - an intentionally false statement a) used with reference to a situation involving deception or founded on a mistaken impression

False | adj
- not according with truth or fact; incorrect
- appearing to be the thing denoted; deliberately made or meant to deceive
- illusory; not actually so
- treacherous; unfaithful

Fact | noun - a thing that is indisputably the case
- used in discussing the significance of something that is the case
- a piece of information used as evidence or as part of report or news article

In a world filled with instant access, we have become know-it-alls overnight. Thus, the battle for truth is now waged upon the edge of a knife, which consequently I'm holding and hoping to stick you with. Truth and Untruths. Fact and Fiction. Truth and Lies. These ideals tip the scales for acceptance, autonomy, and application. Yet, none of that matters until others see what we see as TRUTH, even if our ideal truth is only wrapped up in our level of exposure; perhaps even wrapped up in the easily attainable lie or lukewarm lie that I've come to believe as truth. Whether you like it or not, our "truth" is subjective.

Based on the definitions of "true" or "false," in order for us to discover truth/untruth, we need first to take a look at the facts. Over the next few chapters, you'll find some facts of the Bible on a handful of topics to discover the truths and untruths that we as the body of Christ have come to accept.

If facts are the measure of truth, then our level of truth is only based upon our exposure to facts, and if the facts we've been exposed to aren't the fullness of truth, then our truth is lacking. This is a big problem in the world as we know it today. The world as we know it buys into the lie that if "I believe it, that means you have to believe it too." It's not enough for it only to be our truth, we desperately want others to acknowledge that this is their truth as well. Otherwise, we'll label "someone" a simpleton who hasn't come into the knowledge that we now hold.

Just because something is true doesn't mean that it meets the standard of truth. This is a dangerous and slipperiest of slopes to live on. This ideal gives us the excuse that we don't have a need for ultimate truth. In the discovery of what is true and untrue, we need to hold the idea of our truth versus their truth loosely. There is only one Ultimate Truth, and that is the truth of who God is and the truth of what He knows and has known from the beginning, all the way till the end. If it's safe to say that God is the only one who knows absolute truth, then that must mean even our interpretation of His truth can be suspect to some lukewarmness. This is where the chasm lies between *the* truth and *our* truth ... between truth and untruth ... and this is where lukewarm lies fester.

Half of a lie is a lie ... And half of a truth is also a lie. But, if that lie is passive enough, not being too hot (that it scalds my tongue) or too cold (where it hurts my teeth), it may be palpable enough to accept because of its lukewarm nature.

Take the word "sin" for instance, which means to miss the mark. If we are holding onto a half-truth of what Scripture says ... does that mean we could be missing the mark? If so, then is it possible that we would sacrifice relationship with Him in order to keep our version of what we deem as "true"? Could we be missing the mark and end up with a theology that's lukewarm?

If all we've ever been shown is a partial Gospel, to come into contact with the full truth of the Gospel might lead us to mistake it for a lie, and claim that it's only half true. Ironically, standing on a foundation of "half-truths" leads me to go into battle against the enemy half-cocked, and fully exposed.

Let's take a dive into a few examples in Scripture where we may have substituted the truth for a lie—maybe just a lukewarm lie. In doing so, I hope to awaken an appetite within you, so that you can seek the Word of God for yourself.

Before we begin, as a sign of authority, would you be willing to place your right hand over your heart and pray this prayer with me? In order to go after the foundations, we want to give God permission to enter in ... give our hearts permission to grant Him access. Hand over heart ... Right hand, please ... Say out loud:

Heart! I give you permission to ask questions, seek answers, and walk with an open attitude, so that I might accept what the Lord has for me throughout this journey.

Father God, I give you permission to enter into the lukewarm places so that You can fill me with Your truth. Walk with me as I read and allow Your revelations to take root inside of my soul. Amen.

CHAPTER ONE

BOUGHT
&
PAID FOR

Meeting my wife was like sticking a paper-clip into an electrical socket— instant flow of energy frying everything within me. From the moment we met, we were discussing and diving deeply into the things of God—Holy Spirit, Scripture, Prophecy, Tongues, you name it. If it could be talked about we covered it. Our first date, which started as the MOST awkward double date (with her aunt and uncle) turned into a six hour discussion that would drastically change the course of our lives.

Growing up, my family was all about the power and indwelling presence of the Holy Spirit. My parents taught me how to have a prayer language at a young age, and I was extremely sensitive to what was going on around me. Though, over the years we began to let lying dogs lie, instead of rounding up the hounds for the hunt of life. That's not to say that we weren't spiritual in nature or that we stopped going to church or that we didn't create intimacy with God. Like most Americans, technology became my altar of sacrifice, giving more and more of my time to movies, video games and TV and less time to prayer and spiritual discussion. The enemy enjoys using "Media" and our need for advancing technology to dull our senses and lull us into a false sense of security. I still prayed. I was still active in our church, but I didn't go after the things we used to when I was a child.

Back to the circuit breaker that is now my wife. If there was a whiff of the supernatural, she wanted it. Somewhere along the way, I bought into the elitist mentality that my "schooling" entitled me to the opinion that I was right and the rest of the world was wrong. I was very popular (wink, wink). I'd like to blame my schooling, but it couldn't have possibly been my own highly opinionated, strong-willed and slightly dominating personality, could it? Regardless, our first few years of marriage were filled with my wife diving into the deep end of the spiritual pool and me sitting in the lifeguard chair, warning her of the dangers of diving boards, lack of oxygen, head trauma, waiting 30 minutes after eating before swimming, etc.

The last seven years of marriage have been a low and slow burn of my reluctant heart to recognize that I might not have all the answers. As I began to study the scripture (that I had been tested on and reviewing for "years"), I saw a side of God, Jesus and Holy Spirit that I hadn't seen before. Brokenness from my home life skewed my view of God. Because of my own dysfunction, I couldn't walk in the fullness of who God made me to be.

What were some of my half-truths? I'll give you an example. A running joke in my family, and by joke I mean everyone else laughing at the personal anguish I went through, is the time my brother hit me with a badminton racket. We were playing in the backyard of our townhome. If I remember correctly, this was a new set of racquets that I had gotten as a gift. My big brother (we'll call him Jefferson) and I went out to play. As most outings would have it, Ole Jeffy and I got into it. One thing led to another, and I demanded the racquet be returned to me. He gave it to me, alright. From across the yard, he chucked the surprisingly aerodynamic piece of swift justice at me and BAM. My lights go dark, I go down, hands come away from my face, and there is blood. By his recollection, it was merely a drop. To my young, now traumatized eyes, there was "a river of life flowing out of me," but it was not helping the lame to walk nor the blind to see. Eventually, the eye was bandaged by my dad, though the scar remains.

Where's the half-truth? I knew growing up my brother loved me (obligation) and that he spent time with me (proximity). Yet obligation and proximity don't exactly give anyone the warm fuzzies, much like the proximity of cold steel to your cheek. I know Jesus loves me (obligation) and that He spends time with me (proximity). He lives in me now. It's not like we can be mutually exclusive. But, just because we're close, by spatial reasoning, doesn't mean He actually values who I am, does it?

Does He really love me enough to walk through tough times with me? Here Lies my half truth. I'm pretty sure He loves me, but the problem is I'm not so sure He really enjoys spending time with me

I'm the one who's chipping away at the great divide because I've come to believe a lie about Jesus. Of course, He loves me, but He has to. Of course, He'll spend time with me but only if He's not busy. I know a portion of His character, but the lack in my own reveals the insecurity that's been bred by my physical relationships and these lies are now trickling over into my spiritual realities.

When my lack of revelation comes into contact with something that seems "good enough" two things have happened; 1) I've come to judge what's acceptable and what's not and 2) the measurement of the "half-truth", if it seems to balance out with the revelation I've come into contact with thus far, can skew my version of truth.

I know there's power in the cross of Christ, but that's only by means of salvation. I can't be trusted with power. I know God is a good Father, but where was He when Jesus needed Him? Where was He when I needed Him? I know some sweet things happened in the book of Acts, but I don't see those things happening today so when someone says "that died with the Apostolic age" I don't buck at that assumption.

The problem is my level of truth is relative to my exposure. Notice I didn't say God's truth is relative, but I will say my understanding of His truth can be. If God is the fullness of all truth, it is absolute arrogance to come to any conclusion that says I understand the full measure of who God is and what He means through His scriptures.

Now, this brings up an interesting crossroads. One passage says that we can understand the mind of God for we have the Spirit of God, while another passage says that we only see in part, eventual in whole. Regardless of where you stand on this issue, even Christ did not claim equality with God something to be grasped, yet He humbled Himself. The beginning of wisdom is humbling myself to know that the further I engage the Kingdom of God the less and less I probably know. The best part is that we can ask and we get to ask the only One who really knows.

My revelation of who God can be in me, through me and around me will either limit or free me to an experience. Let me explain. If my only interpretation of Jesus being the "Word" is to turn to the Bible, I can venture into the world that says, "Jesus only speaks to us through the Bible." Now don't hear me saying that we shouldn't read the Word, but *the Word* is not a book. The Word is the person of Jesus Christ. The Word (the book) is there to help us understand the Word (Christ), so we can come into relationship with Him. It's through Jesus that we learn the tone, voice, and character of the One who is speaking.

Time and time again in the New Testament the person of Jesus Christ is engaging His people in order to do great things for the Kingdom. In John 20:30, it mentions there are not enough books in all the world to contain all that Jesus did in His three-and-one-half years of ministry. If the man-made, God-breathed, printed text that's on your bedside table is only a highlight reel of Jesus' exploits on earth, doesn't it go to show that God might still be capable of so much more?

It's so easy to buy into the mainstream current of modern day Christianity, but the price ends up being more than we can bear. What's already bought and paid for in your life?

No, I'm not talking about a house or a car. I'm talking about what have you bought into that's a lukewarm lie, and you are now paying for it? The cost of a lukewarm gospel leaves the church either full of truth (arrogance) or full of grace (sissies); full of passion (egotistical) or full of reverence (fast asleep); full of signs and wonders (mystical) or full of studying (practical). But what if Christ never came to purchase us for a watered down version of life? What if His life didn't just pay for us to go to heaven so we could spend eternity with Him, but was proof that with God we can walk in power before we ever get there? It's time for the body of Christ to put their money where their faith is. It's time to make sure this life is bought and paid for. It's time to know what it is we're buying into so we can understand the cost when we're paying for it.

The following chapters are not in sequential order. If you'd like to flip around and hit specific topics, by all means, this book is yours. But before passing it up, make sure to stop in at every mark along the yardstick. Measure it yourself. Come to find out what you can by taking these thoughts and comparing them to what you see in Scripture. This is not a complete work of the mysteries of God; this is just the diving board to get you into the deep end. Are you ready to dive in? Take a deep breath. Here we go.

CHAPTER TWO

BEFORE THE CROSS

AMAZING WOOD ... HOW SWEET THE SOUND

A few weeks ago, my Rib (You know Adam and Eve ... come on?) and I were discussing Biblical things (We don't talk about TV series or other mundane stuff, we discuss theology. I know ... pray for us.) We discovered something. Jesus raised people from the dead before He, Himself, was raised. Jesus healed blind eyes, deaf ears and lame bodies before the resurrection. Yes, there is power in the resurrection of Christ to defeat sin, but what if the power isn't in the cross? What if it's in the One who chose the cross? Talk about a paradigm shift. We as a body wouldn't have to look to a refurbished piece of wood as our standard any longer because our standard would become Christ. Check it out:

Fixing our eyes on Jesus, the pioneer and perfecter of faith.
For the joy set before Him He endured the cross, scorning its
shame, and sat down at the right hand of the throne of God.
Hebrews 12:2 (NIV)

This Man was handed over to you by God's deliberate plan
and foreknowledge, and you, with the help of wicked men,
put Him to death by nailing Him to the cross.
Acts 2:23 (NIV)

Having canceled the charge of our legal indebtedness, which
stood against us and condemned us; He has taken it away,
nailing it to the cross.
Colossians 2:14 (NIV)

So Jesus said, "When you have lifted up the Son of Man, then you will know that I am He and that I do nothing on My own but speak just what the Father has taught me."

John 8:28 (NIV)

Jesus didn't say, "When you lift up the cross ...." He said, "When you lift up the Son of Man." There is no power in the wood. There was a transaction *on* the wood, but the power lies in the one who hung on an instrument of torture. Hebrews 12:2 says, that "He endured the cross." If there's power in the wood why would He have to endure it? Consider that what needed to be endured is not the instrument of our salvation, but simply the platform upon which my Lord gave of Himself in an exchange of our filth for His righteousness.

BEFORE THE CROSS

For the sake of space and time, here's a highlight reel of some of the miracles Jesus performed before the cross.

- Water into Wine - John 2:1-11
- Heals Official's Son - John 4:43-54
- Drives Out Evil Spirit - Mark 1:21-27, Luke 4:31-36
- Heals Peter's Mother-in-Law - Matt 8:14-14, Mark 1:29-31, Luke 4:38-39
- Heals Many Sick and Oppressed - Matt 8:16-17, Mark 1:32-34, Luke 4:40-41
- Miraculous Catch of Fish - Luke 5:1-11
- Cleanses a Man with Leprosy - Matt 8:1-4, Mark 1:40-45, Luke 5:12-14
- Heals Centurion's Paralyzed Servant - Matt 8:5-13, Luke 7:1-10

- Roof Entry Paralytic Healed - Matt 9:1-8, Mark 2:1-12, Luke 5:17-26
- Heals a Man's Withered Hand (Sabbath) - Matt 12:9-14, Mark 3:1-6, Luke 6:6-11
- Raises a Widow's Son from the Dead - Luke 7:11-17
- Calming the Storm - Matt 8:23-27, Mark 4:35-41, Luke 8:22-25
- Casts Demons into Pigs - Matt 8:28-33, Mark 5:1-20, Luke 8:26-39
- Heals Woman in Crowd with Issue of Blood - Matt 9:20-22, Mark 5:25-34, Luke 8:42-48
- Raises Jairus's Daughter Back to Life - Matt 9:18,23-26, Mark 5:21-24,35-43, Luke 8:40-42,49-56
- Heals Two Blind Men - Matt 9:27-31
- Heals a Man Who Was Mute - Matt 9:32-34
- Heals Invalid in Bethesda - John 5:1-15
- Feeds 5,000 (plus Women and Children) Matt 14:13-21, Mark 6:30-44, Luke 9:10-17, John 6:1-15
- Walks on Water - Matt 14:22-23, Mark 6:45-52, John 6:16-21
- Heals Many Sick as They Touch His Garment - Matt 14:34-36, Mark 6:53-56
- Heals Gentile Woman's Demon-Possessed Daughter - Matt 25:21-28, Mark 7:24-30
- Heals a Deaf and Dumb Man - Mark 7:31-37
- Feeds 4,000 (plus Women and Children) - Matt 15:32-39, Mark 8:1-13
- Heals Blind Man at Bethsaida - Mark 8:22-26
- Heals a Man Born Blind (Spit) - John 9:1-12
- Heals a Boy of Unclean spirit - Matt 17:14-20, Mark 9:14-29, Luke 9:37-43
- Miraculous Temple Tax in Fish's Mouth - Matt 17:24-27
- Heals a Blind, Mute Demoniac - Matt 12:22-23, Luke 11:14-23
- Heals a Woman Crippled for 18 Years - Luke 13:10-17

- Heals Man with Dropsy on Sabbath - Luke 14:1-6
- Cleanses Ten Lepers on the Way to Jerusalem - Luke 17:11-19
- Raises Lazarus from the Dead - John 11:1-45
- Restores Sight to Bartimaeus - Matt 20:29-34, Mark 10:46-52, Luke 18:35-43
- Withers Fig Tree on the Road - Matt 21:18-22, Mark 11:12-14
- Heals a Servant's Severed Ear - Luke 22:50-51

If all of these events went down before the cross, then what's the point? Jesus died so that we might have life (and life eternal with Him) but before that Jesus lived a life of power (pre-cross). This means we can live a life of power now, not tomorrow's now, but now's now! On this side of Heaven. He fully relied on God. Fully man. Fully invested in what He heard the Father saying. Only doing what He sees the Father doing. All before He is glorified back into His perfect state.

What am I saying? Is it possible Jesus lived in submission to His family to show us how to grow in maturity and wisdom? Yes! Is it possible that Jesus died and rose to life so that we might have eternal life? Absolutely yes! But is it also possible that Christ led a supernatural ministry for 3.5 years, before glorification, to model for us "on earth as it is in Heaven"? My answer to you is an unequivocal YES!

If we say Jesus is the miracle Man; Baptists, Methodists, Catholics, Charismatics; everyone will say "glory and hallelujah." But the second we attach Holy Spirit's name to ours and say we now have the power to perform miracles, there's a huge split, and some call it demonic, and some shout back in anger. Thus, we get wrapped up in the wrong thing. But Jesus Himself said:

*I tell you this timeless truth: The person who follows me in faith, believing in me, **will do the same mighty miracles that I do—even greater miracles than these** because I go to be with my Father! For I will do whatever you ask me to* *do when you ask me in my name. And that is how the Son will show what the Father is really like and bring glory to him. Ask me anything in my name, and I will do it for you!* (Emphasis added)

John 14:12-14 (TPT)

Here's another little nugget. This one falls right in line after verse 14:

Loving me empowers you to obey my commands. And I will ask the Father, and he will give you another Savior, **the Holy Spirit of Truth**, *who will be to you a friend just like me— and he will never leave you. The world won't receive him because they can't see him or know him. But you will know him intimately because he will make his home in you and will live inside you. (Emphasis added)*

John 14:15-17 (TPT)

Jesus was stoked to leave earth. The disciples were not so thrilled. But Jesus let them know, 'I've got to go to the Father! Trust me. If I go, you can ask anything in My name, and it will be done. Guess what? I'm going to ask Pops to send you Me, in the downloadable version—an upgrade of hardware for software— so that you can have Me wherever you go! When He comes, you will be empowered to do what we've been doing!'

POST-CROSS JESUS

Let's recap for a moment. Christ died and rose again so that we might be sealed for eternity. Are we on the same page there?

He has created a bridge for us to join Him in paradise. Unfortunately, those caught up in the world have been made blind, deaf, and dumb to the things of the Kingdom. They don't see the bridge. This is why signs and wonders are in the world today. It's why Jesus operated in the miraculous when

He was on the earth, and why He continued to do so after His resurrection.

Second Miraculous Catch of Fish - John 21:4-11
Peter's Restoration - John 21:15-17
Saul's Conversion - Acts 9:1-9
Ananias' Mission - Acts 9:10-19
Peter's Vision - Acts 10:9-16
John's Letter - Revelation

If Jesus is the same yesterday, today and tomorrow that means that if He was a miracle worker, in the beginning, walking the earth as a Man performing signs and wonders, then we can conclude that He is still in the miracle making business and that He wants His brothers and sisters to operate in the way He sees His Father operating.

Let's debunk the miraculous for a moment. Are there wonders that take place like missing fingers growing back? Yes. Finances miraculously appearing? Yup. Legs growing out, memories being restored, and physical hearing coming back? Amen and Hallelujah. But this is not the limit to God's miraculous. Every time a broken and bruised heart decides to let down its offenses and step out from behind its defenses, God has just performed a miracle. They had a heart of stone, and now they have a heart of flesh.

For anyone who can't see the hope set before them in life (they may be teetering on the edge of suicide), the moment they see a family member flash before their eyes, or find a career path, or a future spouse, or maybe they just hear the voice of a Father calling out to them above all the noise and confusion; they discover hope, and blind eyes have just been opened. That's a wonder.

Then there's the person with the rejection mindset who says, "I'll always be abandoned." When they come into contact with the loving and restoring power of Jesus Christ they are delivered from a lifetime of pain and are carried into an eternity of love and peace; that's supernatural.

Hebrews 2:3-4 (TPT) says:

The Lord himself was the first to announce these things, and those who heard Him first hand confirmed their accuracy. Then God added His witness to theirs. **He validated their ministry with signs, astonishing wonders, all kinds of powerful miracles, and by the gifts of the Holy Spirit, which he distributed as he desired** (Emphasis added).

Signs and wonders are God's witness being added to the story. This is sneaky Jesus. God, who knows all, wants to use details only known by the individual to meet them exactly where they are. It seems weird, right? But Jesus called out Zacchaeus' name as He just strolled into town. Warning: "Word of Knowledge" sighting in the Gospel. The time Heaven's Son called out the multiple men in the Samaritan Woman's history that she wasn't wed to. Notice: This was a "Word of Knowledge" in the Gospel. Her response was "Come meet a man who told me everything I ever did." He read her mail, and she said thank you. Jesus fed 5,000+ people on a hillside with five loaves and two fish. Notice: Miracle in the Gospel. Casting out demons. Warning: Deliverance ministry in the Gospel. Healing the sick. Notice: You are seeing healing in the Gospel. Jesus is baptized by the Holy Spirit and hears an audible voice from heaven. Notice: This is the Baptism of the Holy Spirit in the Gospel, accompanied by God speaking to a Man.

If it's in the Gospel and it's in the Word; as Hebrews testifies, it's God's way of getting involved in our story. It's time we started looking toward the Father, and what He's up to, more than we look to our theology, pastor, leader, opinion, interpretation or judgment. Isn't it funny how the lukewarm lies we carry are usually filled with judgment?

HOW?

Now that there's a case to look into these things, we can take a look at different portions of scripture as a road map on how to operate in the supernatural instead of looking for excuses on why it "no longer exists." There are not enough words to describe what I'm talking about in fullness. This takes a lifelong pursuit of the things of God. My advice for the meantime is this: Don't seek the miraculous, seek the Miracle Maker. Don't seek healing, seek the Healer. Don't seek provision, seek the Provider. Don't seek favor, seek the Favored One. Don't seek out tongues, seek to speak with Him. Don't seek prophecy, seek His heart for His people.

By seeking out relationship with God, we will come to find who He is, who we are and how we can join Him in what He's up to. When we seek His hand (what He can give us), we'll miss out on His heart (why He wants to give it to us). Learn the heart of God, and you will find everything you're searching for. He wants to walk with you as you learn how to operate His gifts. Who better to teach you? The instruction manual? Or the One who made it! And even wrote the manual! Let's all seek to walk with the "Master Craftsman" when it comes to our lives, giftings, and passions.

Lord, I place my life in Your hands. Shape me. Mold me. Use me. Save me. Keep me. Protect me. I love you, Father. I want to know You more. Reveal to me the mysteries of Your ways so that I can partner with the Kingdom in changing this world. Father work in me before You work through me. I give You permission to search me and find ANYTHING in me that does not reflect Your purity. Refine me in Your love. Refine me in Your passion. And may my heart reflect the heartbeat of Heaven. Amen.

CHAPTER THREE

HOSTING THE GHOST

HOLY WHAT?

God the Father: Totally Cool
Jesus Christ: Rock Star
Holy Spirit: I'm outta here!

Why is the American church so spooked by the Holy Ghost? Over the years I know there's been a lot of brokenness and pain caused in the name of the Holy Spirit, but it's my opinion (and it's OK to have those) that the pain was really caused by people who have been hurt—because hurt people hurt people. And get this, the enemy is absolutely fine with the Holy Spirit getting the blame. Why? Because the enemy is fine with any form of division in the body of Christ and if he can get us twisted when it comes to the Spirit of Jesus, then he can clock out and go home early.

Oh? Have we forgotten that the Holy Spirit is the Spirit of Jesus? Jesus is the Rock Star. But what about the idea that the Holy Spirit is also the Spirit of God? If you remember, God we're totally cool with, and if these ideas are true, why do we get so bent out of shape when it comes to the reigning version of God on the earth? Somewhere along the way, we started drawing lines in the dirt and saying "enough is enough." But the problem is the Holy Spirit isn't to blame; people are.

When our boundaries get crossed, without permission, we get hurt. When we get hurt, we use our pain as an excuse to break away from relationships. When we break away from relationships, we have to have a good reason for why we left. Unfortunately, when good "Christian folk" leave a church there's got to be a really good reason.

Sometimes, it's because "things just got weird," aka: I didn't like the fact that I needed to get vulnerable. Now, I'll start a church where no one needs to get vulnerable, and we'll all hide behind our masks and pretend that nothing's wrong; meanwhile, we're all still hurt, and we have no idea what to do. If only there was a Man who had the power of God that could heal my brokenness from the inside out. Oh, wait, there is! His name is Jesus and He lives in me through the Holy Spirit, but we left Him at that other church. What do we do now?

GHOST STORIES

Living in the deep south for the last few years I've come to realize the power of deep fried food. 1) It's delicious, 2) it's addictive, and 3) you can fry anything. Unfortunately, even though foods are delicious deep fried, it doesn't mean it's good for you. Sometimes, I wonder if we have deep fried the Bible? We only chose what we think tastes good, keep going back for seconds and we cover up the rest.

My favorite memory of late includes a young man named Mac. Two summers ago, his fiancé, now wife, had been baptized in the Holy Spirit. He was out of town for a school co-op for a number of weeks and let's just say this whole thing freaked him out. At this point, I've known Mac for a few years, but he only knew me as the Baptist Student Pastor and not the charismatic, Holy Ghost lover that he was now beginning to "hear" about. Mac ended up avoiding us for a number of months. His fiancé's "experience" was tweaking him out, but instead of coming to talk to the people who were a part of her experience, he decided to talk to anyone and everyone else he could find. Because in Mac's world, "this had to be demonic, and if it wasn't demonic, it surely wasn't biblical."

He later found out his mom had been baptized in the Holy Spirit before he was born. We laugh about that now, but Mac's fiancé was feeling the strain on their relationship, so I did the only thing I could think of. I invited him to our men's bible study—the one where we're studying the book of Acts to see the power and working of the Holy Spirit and how to apply it to 2017. Mac couldn't make it that week. Something about ultimate Frisbee, or something like that. Hey, if you're going to miss a bible study, it had better be for something like ultimate or hacky-sack or something Christian hippies do. Mac eventually ended up coming a week or so later, but he had a ton of questions. That next Sunday he visited our church. A small, interdenominational, fellowship where we follow the leading and prompting of the Holy Spirit. By the end of the service he came up to me, and I asked him what he thought. He nodded his head and said something like, "It wasn't that bad. I liked the worship, and the message was awesome." Somewhere deep in my soul, I chuckled. We continued to talk, and he went on about how he thought it was going to be super weird and full of snakes or something. Heads up, just because someone heard from someone else that a church down the street is different doesn't mean they handle snakes. Please, fact check your sources accordingly.

Anyway, I ended up asking him how he was doing with the whole "his fiancé got dipped in the Holy Ghost" thing and he replied, "I'm not sure." He went on to say how a few years ago a friend in their group in school experienced some of that "stuff" and she ended up hurting a lot of people. "Did she say something to you, or do something inappropriate?" I asked. He said, "No, not really. I know there were some other people who were hurt by it all."

I love Mac's devotion to his friends and their hearts. Unfortunately, Mac had fallen victim to carrying someone else's offense and was stuck with paying the check for something he didn't experience himself. As we continued to talk, Mac said this, "I'm just more focused on having a biblical foundation than all of this other stuff."

Boy, oh boy. Here we go. "Man, me too," I replied. "There are scriptures all over the place talking about the Holy Spirit and the baptism of the Holy Spirit." His eyebrow raised and he said, "really?"

"Of course," I smiled, "I mean, even Jesus was baptized in the Holy Spirit."

"What? Really?"

"Yeah man. In Luke where John baptized Him? When He comes up out of the water, the Spirit descends like a dove and then the clouds part, and God speaks from heaven."

"Wait. What?"

I had no intention of going fishing that day, but that hook sure was sunk. We turned to Luke 3:21-22. After that, we flipped over to Acts 8:14-18 where it says that the people in Samaria were "only baptized in the name of Jesus because He (the Spirit) had not yet fallen on them." Then, as I usually do, I pointed out how John the Baptist AND Jesus mention how John only baptized with water, and how He was going to baptize them with the Holy Spirit and with fire.

A few weeks later Mac came over to my house after small group. He was battling through some anxiety surrounding his work. I ended up asking, "Do you want to be baptized in the Holy Spirit?" He asked why, to which I told him, "This is a daily practice. It's not a one time, one size fits all kind of deal. The Gospel talks about how we now, because of Christ, have access to the Holy Spirit *without measure* (John 3:34). That means there is nothing we can go through that He can't handle. I'm not asking you to drink the Kool-Aid. I'm inviting you to ask for the Comforter—the One Jesus said He was sending to us, to be involved in your life. This is how we have day in and day out relationship with God."

We continued to talk. I showed him some more verses. Eventually Mac opened up his hands, asked for the Holy Spirit to come, and he ended up bowing on the floor and worshipping God.

Mac would say nothing changed for him that night. He, being a skeptic, wasn't even sure if anything had happened at all. He went through the rest of his week questioning the whole experience until something came up at work a few days later. Through a series of unfortunate events, he ended up at home one night, discouraged from work and questioning his identity. Mac didn't realize it, but for the first time, he felt God speaking to him. There wasn't some audible voice, just a feeling deep inside, calming his anxiety, and restoring his peace.

He ended up calling me a day or so after that encounter. Not only had God freed him from anxiety, but he also got a letter in the mail stating that he had been nominated for a prestigious award on campus in his field of study in his graduate program. Not only did God deal with one day's frustration. He showed up and reminded Mac of his value.

That's the point. The Father through the Holy Spirit, wants to restore His children into the model and identity that He created them for. Anxiety, fear, stress, and brokenness are all results of separation from Him. By being baptized in the Holy Spirit, you are exchanging your ability for His. And like I told Mac, "You received the Holy Spirit the moment you got saved. But that's kind of like getting the keys to a car. Until you get baptized in the Holy Ghost, you're just sitting there with keys in your hand. You can get in and out of the car all you want, but if you want to go anywhere, you've got to turn on the power to do so."

Are you holding keys to your destiny? Sitting in the driveway of your calling, frustrated and not going anywhere? I encourage you to crank up the engine by asking the Holy Spirit to come, right now. And just like any car, anytime I want to go somewhere I need to turn on the power. I have no power, but I'm connected and plugged into the source of power! I've got everything I need in Him.

Mac now wants to be an advocate for reconciling those who don't believe in the Holy Spirit and those that do. (Ironically, if you believe in Jesus you believe in the Holy Spirit. The divide is on whether or not the things in Acts are still for today or not. Good thing Jesus' atonement isn't up for debate.)

BORN OF THE SPIRIT

Jesus answered and said to him, "Truly, truly, I say to you, unless one is born again he cannot see the kingdom of God." Nicodemus said to Him, "How can a man be born when he is old? He cannot enter a second time into his mother's womb and be born, can he?" Jesus answered, "Truly, truly, I say to you, unless one is born of water and the Spirit he cannot enter into the kingdom of God. That which is born of the flesh is flesh, and that which is born of the Spirit is spirit. Do not be amazed that I said to you, 'You must be born again.' The wind blows where it wishes, and you hear the sound of it, but do not know where it comes from and where it is going; so is everyone who is born of the Spirit."

John 3:1-8 (NASB)

In order to receive a realm that is, and of itself, spiritual we need to be born of the Spirit. Nowhere in this passage does it say we are to inherit a water realm, or that the Kingdom of heaven is watery. Yes, there is a need to be baptized by water, but there's also a command that is backed up time and time again by Jesus Himself for a baptism of the Holy Spirit. The difference here being, we only need to get dunked in the water once, as an outward profession of our faith in Jesus. I don't know about you, but I need a dose of the Ghost every day, and usually twice on Sunday's! Being baptized in the Holy Spirit is not limited to a one-time thing, because Jesus has access to, as John 3:34 says, "give the Holy Spirit without limitation."

HOLY WAR

The fact is, we need the Spirit in our lives. The issue I've come into contact with is that we haven't been taught how to host the Ghost. We get into these moments of praise; where the

Spirit of God is moving and active and ministering across the body, and then it happens—a tug-of-war and the battle begins. This battle is all up to the leadership in your church and the sensitivity to what could or could not be going on. I've been in worship settings where the band and the pastor were going after the Holy Ghost, but He already left an hour ago. I've also been to worship experiences where people ranted and raved about the power of God moving in the service, and I'm not sure He had been given the right address that morning.

I say all that in fun, but there's a lot of truth to the fact that we can end up quenching the Spirit by ignoring His prompting to linger or even the prompting to move on. Please hear me out. We can't afford to conjure up something that isn't there. Too often, I see in charismatic circles the need to just "let go and let God," but God is a God of order. Check out the tabernacle. God has a place and a plan for utensils. If God cares that much about cutlery, I bet He cares about our service to Him, too.

Now on the flip side of that same coin are the fellowships that carry out the "plan." There's a phrase I hear all too often in the church: "We believe that the Spirit of God was in our meeting last week, and we trust that what we've put together is what needs to be done Sunday." That is absolutely correct. Based on a Thursday meeting and based on what God has been doing in your meeting that day, this plan is exactly what needs to be done this coming weekend.

But what happens when a major crisis hits our community? If the plan for Sunday was hype and celebration of the Most High, but all of our people are walking in after the loss of a trusted community leader, is our plan the best option? Some would say, "That's why God planned it out that way. To lift their spirits." But is it more probable that your Thursday plan never included Saturday's tragedy, and now is the time to shift gears?

I love a good plan. I am a Type B personality with a whole lot of Type A in my system. If I don't have a plan, my left eye might start twitching. But what happens when the plan is no longer a part of *the* plan? Are you able and ready to shift gears and take it where the Lord is leading it? Or are we more concerned with the amount of "wasted work" if we were to drop your plan? When it comes down to it, we have to follow what the Lord wants to do and when He wants to do it. If we get to the beginning of a worship service, and we feel like the "plan" is in motion, then let's stick to the plan, but the second that the Spirit starts to hover over a song (much like He hovered over the deep in Genesis 1) and God starts to shine some light on a situation, we have a choice to make. Do we control? Or do we hand it over? The tug of war has begun. The Holy War for a holy moment!

What if God's plan was never about "the plan"? But what if He was using our plan to get us into a posture that was ready to follow Him when He decided to blow on those embers inside our heart? It's much easier to walk out a plan and not have "the Spirit fall" then to count on the Spirit falling without having a backup plan; especially if He decides to stand back and watch that morning. For worship leaders and pastors, I think the Holy War we face is when to give up control in order for Him to do what He wants to do. We can get the plan in progress, but when the plan obstructs progress, we must be ready to follow the One we're here for in the first place.

HOSTING THE GHOST

Jack Taylor says, "How can you fit God, who is everything, into anything?" It's like taking too much soup and trying to stuff it into a Tupperware container. It's not going to work. Our job is not to control what the Spirit of God wants to do. Our job is to host Him. Create a place for Him at the table. Set an atmosphere for Him to move. Give Him permission to do so.

How do we do this? We go after the presence of God. When we go after the presence, we will begin to see a piece of Him who is everything moving in a way that touches anything. How? We make a plan. The plan is to get into the presence by posturing ourselves to meet with Him. Because we were made by Him, we are capable of hosting Him. We are not able to build anything that can contain Him. Yet, He has already made us to be the temple of the Holy Spirit, so when we turn our lives over to Him, we are able vessels ready to be filled.

Mary Buckley, a spiritual mother of mine, says, "The influence a person carries is directly related to their pursuit of God's presence. The impact of a ministry is directly related to its pursuit of God's presence. The lasting effect of a person's life is directly related to the pursuit, understanding, and experience of His presence."

I believe every son and daughter of God has the ability to host the presence at any time and in any place. Try it. Let's try it by turning our affection towards Him. If you need to close your eyes or place a hand over your heart or even lean back; go for it. Invite Him into your world right where you are. You don't need Bethel's newest song. Or an instrumental track in the background. Or a dark room. You are the temple of God! Do It!

Growing up in Virginia Beach I was in training for hosting the presence of God from a young age. I learned more about God out in the ocean than I ever did anywhere else. First of all, a wave is a glimpse into the power of God. Secondly, a wave is the truest expression of creativity in the world. There are no two waves that are alike, though they travel in sets. Thirdly, you don't control the wave. You ride it. Fourthly, your eyes have to be trained on how to spot the sets. Have you ever seen a surfer sitting on the shore just watching the waves? There might be other reasons for that, but usually, they are checking the break and timing the sets.

I thank God that He has trained me on how to recognize the swells of the Spirit and more than that, how to ride them. If you try to make a wave do what you want to do, you will be sucking salt water. Learning how to set up for a wave, catch it and ride it takes more than turning around and waiting. You have to paddle, position yourself and then paddle some more. It's all about posturing yourself. And there's always a level of preparation for the ride. But the plan? The plan is to go with the flow.

As worship leaders, are we getting smacked around by the torrent of mistakes and miscommunications with our worship teams on a regular basis? Maybe it's time to sit on the shore and observe the flow.

As pastors, do we feel like every week we get right to the edge of what God is doing only for our team to bail out and move on to the next song? Maybe it's time to show our worship leaders how to posture themselves for where we're intending to go. And maybe there needs to be a little more preparation (or paddling) in order to get there. What we plan for is what we'll get, unless we allow the Spirit to move.

Church members, remember not to judge someone who's in the water when we're still on the shore. Currents are a funny thing. On the surface, everything can appear one way, while simultaneously a riptide is carrying them away. These waves that I'm talking about, in the Spirit, are a privilege to ride and take a lifetime to enjoy. His presence is powerful, creative, unique (every time), uncontrollable and it travels in sets. How we set ourselves up (plan), paddle (prepare) and lean in (posture) will determine whether or not you're hosting the Ghost.

CHAPTER FOUR

THE DISTANT FATHER

LUKEWARM LIES

By now, hopefully, you've started to see that things in Christianity are not as they seem. As we gaze at the title of this chapter, you're probably starting to skip a few pages wondering where this one is going.

Before we venture any further, it needs to be said: God is good. This is a truth, the whole truth and nothing but the truth. Why does it seem so shallow, though? Why does it feel as if we're being baited? It seems shallow because our version of truth is relative to our exposure (Chapter 1). It seems that we're being baited ... because we are. Remember that there are many truths in the Gospel of Christ and that there are many lukewarm lies in the church today. Somewhere along the way, we decided to buy into quick fixes to big problems and viola, theologies were made—theologies like this one.

THE ROMANS ROAD

I wonder if those who came up with the "Romans Road" realized that they created a half-truth theology that would trap Christians in bondage rather than freeing them; which was its original purpose. For those of you who don't know what the Romans Road is, it's a number of passages from the book of Romans to help lead people to salvation in Jesus. Here it is:

- **Romans: 3:23**: "For all have sinned and come short of the glory of God."

- **Romans 6:23**: "For the wages of sin is death; but the gift of God is eternal life through Jesus Christ our Lord."

- **Romans 5:8**: "But God demonstrates His own love toward us, in that while we were still sinners, Christ died for us."

- **Romans 10:9**: "That if you confess with your mouth Jesus as Lord and believe in your heart that God raised Him from the dead, you will be saved."

- **Romans 5:1**: "Therefore, since we have been justified through faith, we have peace with God through our Lord Jesus Christ."

Now, these buffet items at the church social are delicious and quite succinct; however, I have one question; "who let Quentin Tarantino make this plotline?" Some add to the *Roman Road:* Romans 10:13, "Whoever calls on the name of the Lord shall be saved" right after Romans 5:8; leaving out Romans 5:1. Regardless of that seemingly insignificant fact, how do you go from Chapter 3 to Chapter 6, back to Chapter 5, jump ahead to Chapter 10, and then land on Chapter 5 again? Paul is writing to the believers in Rome. This is a letter. It's not strips of paper with multiple verses on it, like a Word salad, tossed in a bowl for us to draw at random. This destroys the narrative of the writer and totally breaks down the reason Paul was writing to the Romans in the first place.

This particular book of the Bible was written to ease the tensions in Rome. Emperor Claudius evicted the Jews from Rome (around AD 49), leaving the church bereft of its leadership and forcing the Gentiles to step up to the plate and start leading. When Claudius died, Emperor Nero allowed the Jews back into Rome (around AD 54). It was a great homecoming. Friends and family were reunited. Homes were reestablished. Finally, it was time to set the church back up as it was. The Jews wondered, "What are the Gentiles doing here?" Paul addressed the divide by trying to remind the Gentiles that Israel was God's chosen people. Quickly turning back, he reminded the Jews that all are *only* justified by faith. This was Paul's moment in the political spotlight, as it were, hoping most earnestly that the politics of the church would subside and that those calling themselves Christians would remember what the Kingdom is all about.

- Romans 3:23, "For all have sinned and fallen short ..." This is a verse written to the Jews, who thought they were entitled to God's love because they were a chosen people. They thought that the Gentiles were the only ones who had "sinned."

- Romans 6:23, "For the wages of sin is death ..." Gill's Exposition explains that sin, in this portion of Scripture, is denoted as a king and death was the wage for serving this particular king. This is again referring to the Jews and their belief system. Paul is trying to unclasp their fingers from around the Law and remind them that, "the gift of God is eternal life through Christ Jesus our Lord."

- Romans 5:8, "While we were still sinners, Christ died for us ..." This verse reveals the open salvation over all who come into a relationship with Jesus. We "were" sinners, now saved by Christ. Does sin still exist in the world today? Yes, but the open pardon over every Christian's life means that as soon as we dip our feet in the world, Christ has dipped them back into the blood. Through Adam, we all sinned. Through Christ, we have all been pardoned.

- Romans 10:9, "If you confess with your mouth Jesus is Lord ..." We come into a relationship with Him; turn from the death we inherited in sin and walk in the life He offers, having been raised from the dead; so we in turn are raised.

- Romans 5:1, "Since we have been justified through faith …" When we read this part of the verse, we can start to believe that it is faith that justifies us. Unfortunately, there are many today who believe it is faith, and faith alone, that justifies us. God, through Christ's sacrifice and resurrection, has justified us. It is by choosing to believe in this mighty work of God that we are saved by faith. If it were by faith that we were saved, then it is by *our* work that we are saved. We are saved by Christ and Christ alone. Our faith in the One who saves us is what justifies us.

Here's an example: If my father gave me $1 Million (wink, wink) and I believe that he'll do it, then I have faith that the money will be mine. My faith in the transaction doesn't mean the money is mine. My dad is the one giving the money, so my faith is resting on his promise.

Back to the Roman's Road. Do you see the disconnection? Do you see the dissension? Paul is directing the first two verses of the Roman Road toward the Jewish believers who were still preaching a law and works and chosen race. A much more accurate "Roman Road" would be dropping those verses and holding fast to the last three; this way there is only a clear picture of what God has done for us.

I say all this because every time it's mentioned that we are sons and daughters of God, or that we inherit the Kingdom, or that we are blameless in Christ; without fail there is some legalist in the group that says, "For all have sinned and fallen short!" I think to myself, "Thanks, Alfred. Are we in the synagogue? Do I have a goat in my hands?"

In Bible College I was told to look at Scripture from four vantage points, 1) The Literal Sense, 2) The Allegorical Sense, 3) The Moral Sense and 4) The Anagogical Sense. These are broken up into two different groups:

1. Literal
   a. Exegesis
   b. Critical explanation or interpretation of the text
2. Spiritual
   a. Allegorical
      (1) Symbols that allude to later events
      (2) Ram for Abraham = Jesus for us
   b. Moral
      (1) How we should act
      (2) Prodigal Son Story = My acceptance of those that come back
   c. Anagogical
      (1) Points to future events
      (2) Book of Revelation = What's to come

The point is, we shouldn't only take scripture at face value for what it says. We are to examine in a multidimensional fashion that which Christ (the Word) is trying to teach us through relationship and His living Scriptures.

Something I realized as well, if you stopped reading halfway through a book and tried to summarize the intent of the author based on limited facts, you would be making a limited assessment. Why then, do we continue to preach "sin" in a world that has already been rid of it, especially in the church? If Christ has died for sin, once and for all, why do we still hold people to a measuring rod of sin, when Christ has already broken it? I fear the Romans Road has been so ingrained into some generations that we have brainwashed them into a lukewarm theology where Christ loves you, only if you're perfect. How can you be perfect? Don't sin. Once you do, uh oh!

SIN

Do Christians still sin? Yes. Are we still sinners? No. Before you shut this book; let me explain: I have two brothers. They're my brothers because they were left by their birth mother on a train, heading into Kiev, Ukraine. They were four and five years old—abandoned, alone, and forgotten. Somehow Sergei, (now Will) took care of Valera (affectionately referred to as James) and they survived the streets of Kiev. I don't know if we'll ever know the length of time they spent there. Eventually, the police took them to a safe haven, called The Ark—a Christian Care Center for Kiev street children and rehabilitation center for broken families. There, they were rehabilitated, counseled, and walked through spiritual healing for many of the traumas they'd been through. Long story short, my parents met Sergei and Valera, fell in love and they are now Will and James Kuenzli.

Using my brother's story, are they orphans? Are they sons? They *were* orphans, but they are now sons. There is a legal document that says my parents cannot unadopt these boys. With their birth certificates being changed, it is as if they were born to us!

A verse I think that should be implemented into the Romans Road is this:

And you did not receive the "spirit of religious duty," leading you back into the fear of never being good enough. But you have received the "Spirit of full acceptance," enfolding you into the family of God. And you will never feel orphaned, for as He rises up within us, our spirits join Him in saying the words of tender affection, "Beloved Father!

Romans 8:15 (TPT)

For you have not received a spirit of slavery leading to fear again, but you have received a spirit of adoption as sons by which we cry out, "Abba! Father!"

Romans 8:15 (NASB)

A DISTANT FATHER

"OK," you say, "But what about the fact that God can't look on sin?"

Where does it say that?

You might say, "The fact that Adam and Eve were kicked out of the Garden because of sin ...."

True. But did God say, "Eww. You sinned. Get out?"

"No. Not exactly."

He said, "Now, man is like us, knowing good from evil. So that he doesn't take from the tree of life, eat from it, and live forever." Because of this, God sent him out of the Garden.

"Because they sinned right?"

It never clarifies that. We can jump to that conclusion but based on what God spoke through His Word, we can conclude that man felt shame (naked) and the woman blamed (the serpent). So that they wouldn't live in shame and blame forever, God excused them from the Garden to protect the tree of life. Isn't it funny that Christ died on a "tree" and that He leads to life? But since shame and blame miss the mark of God's true intent for us, we can call it sin.

You may be wondering, "If sin didn't expel Adam & Eve from the Garden then why does God hate sin? Doesn't the Bible say that God is unable to look on sin because He turned away from Jesus on the cross?"

Mmm ...

"Why does God hate sin?"

What do you mean?

"He can't look on it!"

Says who?

"The Bible."

Where?

"When He turned away?"

What?

"When God turned away?"

But where does it say that?

Aha!

Let's take a look at Matthew 27:45-46.

Now from the sixth-hour, darkness fell upon all the land until the ninth hour. About the ninth hour Jesus cried out with a loud voice, saying, "Eli, Eli, lama sabachthani?" that is, "My God, My God, why have You forsaken Me?"

Matthew 27:45-46 (NASB)

"See ... God *did* turn His back on Him!" you may say. And why? Because you've probably been told that it was at that moment, all of the sins of the world fell on Him as He asks why His Father has abandoned Him.

How do you figure that?

"Cause at that moment all the sins of the world fell on Him. He asks why His Father has abandoned Him."

But where does it say that all the sins of the world fell on Him?

He Himself bore our sins in His body on the cross, so that we might die to sin and live to righteousness; for by His wounds you were healed.

1 Peter 2:24 (NASB)

Surely our griefs He Himself bore, and our sorrows He carried; yet we ourselves esteemed Him stricken, smitten of God, and afflicted.

Isaiah 53:4 (NASB)

"Yeah. See ... there it is," you may say.

If He paid for sin by "His wounds" than did He become sin? Or did He just make the payment?

"I guess He made the payment."

Let's get back to God turning His face away from His Son. Doesn't it feel like He's a Distant Father?

This is a conversation I've had a number of times with so many Christians in the church. I first had this conversation with Johnny Buckner, one of my spiritual fathers. The only exception to it is that he was asking the questions and I was the confounded, firm in my "theology," pupil learning that my view of God was distorted.

"Twinkle, twinkle little star ..."

Did you join in with:

"How I wonder what you are.
Up above the world so high.
Like a diamond in the sky.
Twinkle, twinkle little star.
How I wonder what you are."

I haven't gone mental just yet. Remember that verse in Matthew 27? The "My God, My God, why have You forsaken Me?" Let's take a look at Psalm 22 (Emphasis Added).

My God, My God, why have You forsaken me? Far from my deliverance are the words of my groaning. O my God, I cry by day, but You do not answer; and by night, but I have no rest. Yet, You are holy, O You who are enthroned upon the praises of Israel. In You our fathers trusted; they trusted, and You delivered them. To You they cried out and were delivered; in You, they trusted and were not disappointed (v. 1-5).

But I am a worm and not a man, a reproach of men and despised by the people. All who see me sneer at me; they separate with the lip, they wag the head, saying, "Commit yourself to the Lord; let Him deliver him; let Him rescue him because He delights in him."

Yet You are He who brought me forth from the womb; You made me trust when upon my mother's breasts. Upon You I was cast from birth; You have been my God from my mother's womb. Be not far from me, for trouble is near; for there is none to help. Many bulls have surrounded me; strong bulls of Bashan have encircled me. They open wide their mouth at me, as a ravening and a roaring lion. I am poured out like water, and all my bones are out of joint; My heart is like wax; it is melted within me. My strength is dried up like a potsherd, and my tongue cleaves to my jaws, and You lay me in the dust of death. For dogs have surrounded me; a band of evildoers has encompassed me; **they pierced my hands and my feet. I can count all my bones.** *They look, they stare at me;* **they divide my garments among them, and for my clothing they cast lots** *(v 9-18).*

But You, o Lord, be not far off; O You my help, hasten to my assistance. Deliver my soul from the sword, My only life from the power of the dog. Save me from the lion's mouth, from the horns of the wild oxen. You answer me. I will tell of Your name to my brethren; in the midst of the assembly, I will praise You. You who fear the Lord, praise Him; all you descendants of Jacob, glorify Him and stand in awe of Him, all you descendants of Israel. **For he has not despised nor abhorred the affliction of the afflicted; nor has He hidden His face from him; but when he cried to Him for help, HE HEARD** *(v19-24).*

From You comes my praise in the great assembly; I shall pay my vows before those who fear Him. The afflicted will eat and be satisfied; those who seek Him will praise the Lord. Let your heart live forever! All the ends of the earth will remember and turn to the Lord, and all the families of the nations will worship before You. For the kingdom is the Lord's and He rules over the nations. All the prosperous of the earth will eat and worship, all those who go down to the dust will bow before Him, even he who cannot keep his soul alive. Posterity will serve Him; it will be told of the Lord to the coming generation. They will come and will declare His righteousness to a people who will be born, that He has performed it (v. 25-31).

Did you see it? It's all over this passage. This is the story of Jesus. When He cried out, "My God, My God, why have You forsaken Me?" It was as if Jesus were singing, "Twinkle, twinkle little star ..." The title for this chapter in The Passion Translation is called "A Prophetic Portrait of the Cross," and in the New American Standard Bible it's called "A Cry of Anguish and a Song of Praise." When Jesus cries out that first line of the Psalm, He is worshipping the Lord! He is essentially crying out to His Father and letting all those around know that "God isn't far from Me!"

Every Hebrew boy (and Pharisee for that matter) would have instantly understood what He meant when He referenced Psalm 22. All of a sudden, the realization of what they had come to know through their knowledge sunk deep into their hearts as they understood that this truly was the Christ. This passage talks about how they mocked Him. How they pierced Him yet broke no bones. They divided his garments and cast lots for His clothing. Then at the end of it all, somehow David taps into a holy moment in worship and sings this psalm which was penned centuries beforehand, capturing the fact that God has not despised nor abhorred the afflicted. He didn't hide His face from Him, but when He cried out to His Father, Daddy heard Him.

I submit to you that God is not afraid of sin. I submit to you that Christ could hold our sins and still be God. I submit to you that this wasn't the moment in history when God turned from His Son. I believe at that moment that the Father's face had never been closer to Him. I can imagine Trinity both agonizing and consoling one another—the Father whispering in Jesus's ear, "It's OK, Son. I'm here. It's going to be OK. I love you Son. I am so proud of You. It's OK Son. I love You. I love You. I love You!"

I believe the church has a broken view of the Father; mostly because we have broken fathers. We would never dream of God turning from His Son if we had not first seen it in our families. Perfection is not the key to relationship. It's the unconditional love of a Father who looks on His son in love; even when He has become the propitiation for all who had sinned. And, yet, the Father is able to bear the weight of those sins on Himself, because Trinity, though individuals, are One. What Christ bears, the Father bears. What the Father bears, the Spirit bears. I believe it's time to step out from under the weight of sin and shame and step into the Spirit of Adoption that is given to us through Christ Jesus. We are no longer separated by death, which is the wages of sin. We are now heirs of an unshakable Kingdom. Because God wasn't shaken by Christ on the cross, He is not and will not be shaken by our struggle with sin. Scripture tells us that,

> *We all experience times of testing, which is normal for every human being. But God will be faithful to you. He will screen and filter the severity, nature, and timing of every test or trial you face so that you can bear it. And each test is an opportunity to trust Him more, for along with every trial God has provided for you a way of escape that will bring you out of it victoriously.*
>
> 1 Corinthians 10:13 (TPT)

We do not serve a dictator who is consumed with perfection. If we did, this whole "relationship" would feel super shallow. And it would be hard to recognize God as a Good Father. But we live in a Kingdom Family with a Father who loves us. We are already holy because He is holy. With Christ living in us, we share in His righteousness and have been redeemed back to the Father.

How can the Lord not stand in the presence of sin, yet talk to Cain? Moses? Saul? David? Judas? Saul? Peter? God has always been capable of standing in the presence of sin. It's the only way that Christ was able to walk around sin and free people from their sins. If Christ could not be near sin, because of the Father's distance from it, then how did He walk on the earth for 33 and a half years? I submit to you that sin does not hold as high a priority with God as it does with the church. Maybe it's time to stop labeling those who are far from God as sinners and start calling them into the Family with us. But if we are still under sin, how can we call them into a family that we know nothing of?

I would even say that since Christ has been slain since the foundations of the world, that sin is not even a word used in heaven. Christ already redeemed us, but our obsession with sin and guilt and shame, like a chain around our neck, caused the Father to send His Son in the physical realm so that there could be a new standard in the earth, and we could be freed from our own bondage to something we've already been freed from. As His blood touched the dust, so it touched our dust. As His words broke through our lies, our words can break through their lies. As His love covered a multitude of sins, our love can cover those who sin around us.

I am well aware of 1 John 1:8 (TPT):

If we boast that we have no sin, we're only fooling ourselves and are strangers to the truth.

But check out 1 John 1:9-10 (TPT):

But if we freely admit our sins when his light uncovers them, He will be faithful to forgive us every time. God is just to forgive us of our sins because of Christ, and He will continue to cleanse us from all unrighteousness. If we claim that we're not guilty of sin when God uncovers it with His light, we make him a liar, and His word is not in us.

I am not saying we don't sin, nor struggle with sin. I am saying that my identity is no longer a sinner, but a son of God. God equips me to endure every test that comes, if I'm still struggling with sin I haven't read 1 Corinthians 10:13; and have not resisted to the point of "shedding blood."

I am a son.

He is a Son.

I have a father.

He has a good Father. And His Dad has never failed, looked away, or given up. He is NOT a distant Father. By our Brother's blood, we are now adopted sons and daughters of the Most High God. In the words of Molly Skaggs, "I'm a son. I'm a daughter of the Most High God. He's got the papers on me!"

CHAPTER FIVE

DEVIL IN
THE DETAILS

It's been said that the enemy's main tactics against Kingdom sons and daughters are 1) lies and 2) fear. As far as my knowledge takes me, I don't think he is capable of creating, because I'm pretty sure a created being isn't equal to its Creator. I don't think he's able to create like God can, but I do think he likes to be creative with what he tells you. If you've believed a lie, he will insert fear that the untruth will become true. If you're filled with fear, he will lie to you about the worst outcome coming to fruition.

The devil loves to run through the details. Sprinkling lies and fear wherever he goes hoping that it takes root somewhere within your heart, soul or mind so he can water it into full-blown paranoia. Realize this: he never makes the lie so cold that it shocks your system, or so hot that it scalds you into never making that mistake again; the genius behind the madness is that he makes it just palatable enough to slip past your defenses so that it just blends in with what you already believe. This is the sentiment of *Lukewarm Lies*.

He's not consumed with who buys what or when, he just wants you to buy into his agenda so division, isolation, and destruction can take place. The worst part is, he knows the Word better than we do. They lived together up in heaven long before we were ever created. He not only knows the Word but he also knows the book we all run to in times of need, and Satan is all game for you believing partial truths about what the Truth has spoken. Like we discovered at the beginning of this venture, a half truth is still a *full lie*.

Unfortunately, the devil loves when we run to the Bible when we're "emotionally compromised" because it's then that our fences can be twisted from a place of wholeness into a place of brokenness. Broken theology is riddled throughout the American Christian church because we've traded in our fences of security for defenses that feel good for the sake of my own understanding. Maybe we've traded the protection of God's purpose for the offenses we carry with us into our "community groups" where we "pray" for those we're upset with. In this scenario our prayer is gossip. We use our Christian slang to justify our lukewarm lies in order to do what we please.

There's another well-worn path the devil loves to walk and tread down every chance he gets, which is scripture regurgitation. One of his favorite places to take us to lunch is the buffet line of verses in the Bible. He loves it when we pick and choose from the smörgåsbord of uncontextualized sentences, plucked from the middle of a thought or explanation that has nothing to do with the verse standing on its own. For too long we've chosen verse by verse theology to disrupt and destroy the goodness of God.

The Bible is written as letters from God to His people, through letters from God's people to His people. The story doesn't end with people still trapped in sin and darkness. The Light, Who is Jesus, has already come. Sin is defeated. Darkness is vanquished. Why then do we still preach an Old Testament theology to a New Testament Church where our sin is ever before me, like David? That's a great verse from Psalm 51. But Psalms is chronologically before Jesus, in time. What about the verse where our righteousness is as filthy rags? That's a great verse in Isaiah 64. But Isaiah is chronologically before the coming of Jesus.

Is it possible that the enemy of our faith wants us to live in a sin-shackled mentality, so we don't walk in our rightful heritage as sons and daughters of the most high God? My answer, if you haven't figured it out yet, is YES!

Check out the devil's tactics in the garden. God has relationship with Adam and Eve. Then the serpent comes, and his first question is not about fruit. His first question is disguised in "did God really say …?" Remember how the devil can't create, but he can get creative? Well, he can't create a false narrative where God spoke, if God didn't speak. He only rears his ugly head when the Father is establishing identity, so he can try to break it before it takes root. God spoke. Now the devil speaks up. He calls into question the very words of God in order to get you to question His voice by using your voice as a megaphone for his own voice.

What about in the wilderness in Luke's gospel? Jesus gets dunked in the water. Holy Spirit baptizes the Son. Then the heavens part and God speaks, "This is My son, in whom I am well pleased." Jesus hasn't even done anything yet, and His daddy is proud of Him. It's been spoken. Everyone in earshot has heard it—even the devil. What does he do with it? "If You really are the Son of God …." The devil is in the details—in every detail. The question is hardly ever the question. The question is a disguise to get you questioning God. If he can get you to question God, he can definitely get you to question yourself. If he can get you to question yourself, then you'll be questioning everyone around you—everyone but the one asking questions.

What did Jesus do with the 10 Commandments?

> *You are to love the Lord Yahweh, your God, with every passion of your heart, with all the energy of your being, with every thought that is within you, and with all your strength. This is the great and supreme commandment. And the second is this: "You must love your neighbor in the same way you love yourself." You will never find a greater commandment than these.*

Mark 12:30-31 TPT

Love God.
Love yourself.
Love your neighbor.

"Love yourself? What? That can't be what it says." If you've believed that you're supposed to Love God and Love your neighbor and that's it; please re-read Matthew 12:30-31.

The breakdown in modern Christianity is that we are "nothing" and that we are only supposed to serve God and everyone else. This message is the type of teaching that has broken sons and daughters, leaving us with a dysfunctional body.

We can only love based on the measure that we are loved and can receive love. If we don't feel loved by God, then we don't love those around us. But if we feel loved by God, then we are able to love those around us. We should always feel loved by God. If we don't, we've believed a lie in the core of who we are.

POWERFUL PRONUNCIATION

It is good that you are enthusiastic and passionate about spiritual gifts, especially prophecy. When someone speaks in tongues, no one understands a word he says, because he's not speaking to people, but to God—he is speaking intimate mysteries in the Spirit. But when someone prophesies, he speaks to encourage people, to build them up, and to bring them comfort. The one who speaks in tongues advances his own spiritual progress, while the one who prophesies builds up the church. I would be delighted if you all spoke in tongues, but I desire even more that you impart prophetic revelation to others. Greater gain comes through the one who prophesies than the one who speaks in tongues unless there is interpretation so that it builds up the entire church.

1 Corinthians 14:1-5 TPT

Before we get into the three Ps of Powerful Pronunciation, let's take some time to sit in 1 Corinthians 14. Most would use this chapter to state that Paul claims that tongues are dead and that he himself says "God would rather you speak five words of a known language instead of a thousand words in tongues." Unfortunately, the same people who quote that one verse from the buffet line forget the beginning of verse 19 where he says, "… However, IN

THE CHURCH ...." Paul isn't condemning tongues, he's simply establishing order for the body of Christ when they come together. These same people are the ones who "tear down" other brothers and sisters in Christ with their own words. "Don't speak in tongues" they claim! "It's demonic!" But it's OK to gossip behind people's backs—cuss, speak curses over people (like "you'll never ...," "no one will ever ...," "who would ever ...")— and tear myself down with negative self-talk. To me, negativity is a "tongue." It's just a little more practiced because it's way more cultivated in our communities, families and friend groups.

Why is speaking in tongues such a taboo topic in the church? Why is prophecy such a taboo topic in the church? I believe the pitfall here is found in the three Ps of Powerful Pronunciation. Somewhere along the way, the church got possessive. And where the church gets tight, the prophets get tighter (if "prophetic" people is a strange term, go ahead and skip to *Chapter 7, Digging with Donkeys* before continuing). Scripture is full of people speaking prophetically on behalf of God:

- Moses
- David
- Isaiah
- Jeremiah
- Ezekiel
- Daniel
- John the Baptist
- Jesus
- Peter
- John
- Paul

Just to name a few. Yet there are large bodies of believers who believe today's prophets are heretics! Why? A majority of Christians in the 21st Century are totally comfortable reading about prophets. They just don't know what to do when they're approached by one. Why? Probably because we're not teaching the body of Christ that prophets are still practicing hearing from God. Many claim to be "Bible-believing Christians," yet sadly, their "believing" and their "living" aren't necessarily measuring up together. It's probably because on a whole the church has turned into Sunday School where we're teaching about the things of God instead of actively living out of the ways of God. To study prophets is great! To memorize verses on prophets is great! But the devil in the details is when we don't want to walk out a lifestyle like a prophet. Pharisees hated the Prophet too. Too soon?

POSSESSING

The first Powerful P is **Possessive**.

Teachers, pastors, elders, deacons, little old ladies who unlock the church, Sunday school teachers, small group leaders, parking attendants, greeters, that guy who sits in the back row, the drummer, servers and the C&E (Christmas & Easter) only crowds have all gotten very possessive when it comes to church. Is it entirely the churches fault? Probably not. I'm not here to talk about the culture, but at the heart of it all, the culture has twisted leadership and "followship."

The church has gotten possessive. Attend MY church. Give to OUR ministry. Don't go to THEIR meeting. Listen to THIS teaching. THAT worship is too much.

Leaders that only trust those who look just like them, talk just like them, and believe just like them aren't leaders! This style of "leadership" is essentially smashing faces on the copy machine and pumping out page after page of self-made photocopies, filling churches with narcissistic mirrors where everyone reflects the beautiful version of their leader's life. This is a power play! This is control! This is disgusting!

Because our leaders model possession is power, what do our congregations replicate? They replicate possession, power, and more so power.

We're supposed to be walking out a doctrine of power, but power in Christ. If we have doctrines of power but it's laced with possessive intent we will cause pain instead of bringing life.

This often happens in prophetic ministry. Whether it's prophetic worship, prophecy, prophetic dance, or prophetic utterances; when it's laced with possessive intent, it can often cause pain instead of healing. What does a possessive prophet look like? "God told me to tell you ABC ... so you need to do XYZ!"

Whoa, whoa, whoa! *"God* told me to tell you?"

First of all, if God told you something about someone, praise the Lamb. Second of all, this is *the* power play of power plays. You just used *the* trump card of Christianity. "God said"makes it to where if we disagree with what they say, then they'll say we are living in disobedience. This is a prime example of a possessive approach to prophecy.

Now. Did God tell you? Share with you? Give you insight? Yes. Does that mean that what you say, how you say it and when you say it is God approved? It depends. Why? Because most of us just like hearing the sound of our own voice and we rarely listen for what God is actually saying. My fear is that we've been taught that being "right" is more important than treating others right.

Let's pause for a minute. Do I believe God speaks today? Absolutely! What I'm getting at here is that we shouldn't use, "God told me to tell you" as a power play so that we can run our own personal agenda. By using God this way, we are trying to obtain authority through *the* authority so that no one can question our authority, or what we have to say. This is where possessive intent muddies the waters of ministry. The truth is that God did speak. We may have taken a step too far and thought that we have the final word that needs to be spoken, and start to run with our agenda instead of God's. See the devil in the detail?

Are there times God speaks to us in a way that needs to be shared specifically? Yes. There are times saying, "God told me to tell you" isn't possessive. The danger is this: because we say "God told me to tell you" and it worked, we might start using it just so people will listen to us. That's possessive. This usually happens when we're trying to appear in the river with God, but the creek we're standing in has dried up. No, God doesn't dry up, but maybe our quiet time has, or our prayer life, or whatever else it was that we placed our hope in.

Most possessive intentions are rooted in offense. When we have been offended by others, it can lead us to start offending others. Possessive prophecy is dangerous because it's more self-focused than God-focused.

PROJECTING

The second Powerful P is **Projecting**.

If possessive intent is used so others have to "listen" to what we say; then the art of projection is used, so others have to "live" how we live. This is another pitfall in the world of pronouncing God's secrets. The art of projecting happens when we see similar characteristics in others' lives that mimic our own. Then we feel that God "has" to be speaking to their situation. This leads us to call out, in them what others have called out, in us, so they can now walk through the steps that we've taken. The devil in the detail here is that we can still be wounded over the possessive nature when someone previously prophesied over us and then allow our hurt to dirty the filter when we look at others. We project our story onto the screen of their lives and try to watch it play out. When others don't follow our cues, we get offended.

Projecting onto others robs us of their uniqueness. When we need others to be walking through our circumstances, we can begin to get possessive with how they need to "fix" their situation. It might be time for us as Christians to stop fixing everyone around us and realize that process, though messy, is beautiful. Others need their process in order to walk through wholeness with God. It's their story—not ours. God is in control. Not us. God is able to heal. He's not concerned with fixing. Fixing is to perfection what projecting is to brokenness. It's vital that we don't project our own pain and brokenness onto others just because they share similarities with us. God may have showed us something about them. If there's a lie found here, it's that we don't need to ask God about what He showed us.

Sometimes we project onto others passively by saying, "Man, you remind me of my friend Jake!" Now we have replaced their story with the one we're telling ourselves. I've just replaced another's story with the story I'm telling myself, which is Jake's story. Now, they work at State Farm and are always wearing red shirts. Instead of projecting, we must give people permission to pronounce who they are, even if they happen to wear a red shirt that day.

PROPHESYING

The third Powerful P is **Prophecy**.

I know what you're thinking, "Caleb. These Ps seem more pathetic than powerful."

I know, right?

If you feel this way, praise God! You've arrived.

Prophecy is all about sharing what God wants to say, the way He wants to say it. Will God speak to us about those around us? Yes! And I hope it's a constant thing! Why? Because God cares about His children and He's always talking! A way to avoid being possessive with what God is saying is to phrase it: "I feel like God is saying" or "I'm learning how to hear from God, is it OK if I practice by sharing what I'm hearing?" Or "God might be saying." Do you see the difference?

A phrase like "God told me to tell you," robs them of the ability to choose whether or not they'd like to receive what we have to say.

"I feel like God is saying" gives them permission to receive or reject what we've said because it's about what *He's* saying. It's quite possible that we heard something from the Lord, but didn't articulate it properly. As we walk in the prophetic we need to operate in humility and grace; leaving room for mistakes and victories.

Prophecy is all about permission. God spoke in Joshua 1 to a young leader telling him to, "Be bold and courageous!" God didn't speak that because Joshua was a cocky son-of-a-gun; but because Joshua may have been worried and insecure. God speaks what's not there. Boldness. Courage. Prophecy is God's ability to speak what people need to walk in His ways!

Will God get creative when He gives you a word for those around you? Yup! When you look at the new guy who walks into a church and he reminds you of, well, you; God might be trying to get your attention. Projecting onto someone is simply seeing what we see and speaking what we know. Prophesying is different. Shawn Bolz says in his book *Translating God*, "Discernment is one step shy of revelation." Discernment is what we see. Revelation is what God has to say about what we see. When we see something that reminds us of someone (even ourselves), it is important to take the time to ask God, "Lord, what are You trying to speak to them?"

Here lies the risk. Here is where our faith meets the road. God wants to use our imagination, emotions, memories, mind, heart, soul, spirit and His Spirit to have a supernatural conversation with us. The best part is He wants to use us to encourage, build up, and comfort those around us—to bring edification to the body of Christ.

It's so easy to rip people apart with negativity; especially if the atmosphere we carry stinks of it. But what would happen if we carried an atmosphere of Heaven? His aroma would infiltrate every inch of our lives and prophecy would become second nature.

When it comes to God speaking today ... if I asked you if God spoke directly or personally to you when you got born again, of course, you would say, "Yes!" But was that it? Did He quit speaking? I don't think so.

There's power in what we pronounce. There's even more power in what God is pronouncing! God is possessive about His children. He projects so we can see what He sees. And we get to prophecy what He's speaking!

Now that's powerful!

GOD IS IN THE DETAILS

Ironically the devil has even hijacked popular quotes. The quote "the devil's in the details" actually originated as "God is in the details." Why did it change? Maybe because we've believed the liar instead of the Father. Jesus's ministry was to set us free from sin and death, but before He ever died on a cross, He was about healing our identity by healing the Father's identity in our lives. The enemy wants to rip down the institution of Kingdom Family by muddying up the waters of love with offenses and defenses. I think it's time we built a fence around our hearts so we can keep the devil and his influence out of our lives and remember the Father.

If we've believed the lie that God doesn't speak today, it's probably because we have believed that God doesn't want to speak to us.

This might be a good time to ask Him what He has to say about that. Take some time right now. Ask God to forgive you for believing that He isn't a good Father. Forgive Him for "being distant." He *hasn't* been distant, but by owning that lie, we can finally uproot it and hand it to Him. When we forgive God (let go of our offenses) and ask Him to forgive us (stepping out from behind our defenses), we can finally begin to see God in the details.

CHAPTER SIX

CRUCIBLE
OF
CELEBRATION

OLD OR NEW

When I was in high school my buddy, Mark and I used to drive up and down Virginia Beach Boulevard, hitting all the Thrift Stores in VB and Norfolk. My mind remembers there being 75 of them, but that's because Mark knew where every single shop was and the best route to use to hit them all. As we traveled through ridiculous traffic to the *actual* 20 or so thrift stores, I discovered the beauty of cheap living with something old, but that was new to me. We found hats, shoes, suits, sweaters, shirts, pants, guitars, amps, keyboards and a ton of other useless things that had been handed down and handed out. It was a paradise.

Bethany and I actually found many of our early furnishings in thrift stores and painted it or reupholstered them. Some of which we still own today. People still ask, "Where'd you get this piece?" It was a junker that had been restored. We actually do that now in our ministry—restoration. It's a big part of the way God has dealt with us, and now we have the privilege of leading people into deeper relationships with Him so they can experience similar stories of fullness in God.

Reading through the Word of God is kind of like finding a sweet retro suit at a thrift store. Yeah, it's been worn before, but now it seems to be new because this is the first time I'm seeing myself in this particular set of pinstripe scripture. It's a beautiful book.

Hebrews 4:12 The Passion Translation says:

For we have the living Word of God, which is full of energy, and it pierces more sharply than a two-edged sword. It will even penetrate to the very core of our being where soul and spirit, bone and marrow meet! It interprets and reveals the true thoughts and secret motives of our hearts.

To read God's Word and not be transformed might be because we're reading words on a page and not engaging with the nature of the true Nurturer.

Social "Media" seems to be the staging point for most of the theological blood baths of the 21st century. With only a screen and a "profile" before me, I can say and do whatever, with no penalty, because somewhere in my brain I can justify "speaking the truth" to a profile. The problem is, there isn't much love accompanying these truths and half the time the truths are more *lukewarm* instead of piping hot. But before I digress, we would never speak to anyone face to face the way we talk about them on social "MEdia" or behind their back. It seems gossip has become a social norm.

THE BUFFET LINE

Ironically the word testament means:

1. A person's will, especially the part relating to personal property
2. Something that serves as a sign or evidence of a specified fact, event or quality
3. A covenant or dispensation (in biblical use)

There is a case to defend definition #1. The Word of God does relate to God's children, but too many people might get upset with the idea of us being "personal property;" let's drop that one for now.

Let's stick with definition #2 for now. The Old and New Testaments "serve as a sign or evidence of a specified fact, event or quality." Yet for some reason, there are plenty who read the Bible as a good story, and a reason to join together on Sundays, but "you start throwing that weird stuff at me, and I'll say it's hocus pocus." We end up using whatever verses we like to defend whatever point we want to make by de-contextualizing the truth's found in God's Word—I've seen it so many times in a variety of topics. Welcome to Buffet Line Christianity. We pick and chose our verses to defend our stances and end up destroying God's Word.

Some will use any old verse we want to defend the idea that, even under the blood of Jesus, we are still sinners. Take Psalm 51:3 NASB for example:

For I know my transgressions, And my sin is ever before me.

And 1 Timothy 1:15 NASB:

It is a trustworthy statement, deserving full acceptance, that Christ Jesus came into the world to save sinners, among whom I am foremost of all.

Or Ephesians 2:8-9 NASB:

For by grace you have been saved through faith; and that not of yourselves, it is the gift of God; not as a result of works, so that no one may boast.

There's also the belief that we aren't supposed to speak in tongues because of what Paul says in 1 Corinthians 14:19 NASB:

I desire to speak five words with my mind so that I may instruct others also, rather than ten thousand words in a tongue.

I'm going to tackle these examples one at a time.

THE BUCK STOPS HERE

Somewhere along the line, we forgot that Christ died for ALL sin once and for all on the cross. When we look at the idea that "David's sin was ever before him …," we have to ask ourselves the question, was David alive before or after the resurrection? I hope we can all agree that David predated Jesus. In light of what has happened in the emptying of the tomb, we will still hold to the teachings of the Old Testament, yet not the nature of that covenant. We have a new covenant (Hebrews 10:16).

One of my favorite half-truths that I've heard today is the fact that "Paul said he was a sinner saved by grace." If you look in your Bibles (or even Google it), you will not find a single verse in any translation that says these specific words. Listed above are two separate verses from 1 Timothy 1 and Ephesians 2. Someone decided that both of these verses needed to be lumped together and like sheep we've been led astray. Trying to find the origin of such an audacious claim is difficult, but I'm sure it was a Gaither-type song that caught on a little too deep for the certain denominations to let go.

Chapter 7 is going to take a much deeper look into 1 Corinthians 14, but for now, we need to recognize that oftentimes verse 19 gets taken out of context; much like I quoted it earlier. We forget to read the beginning of verse 19 which says, "however, in the church …." Paul is not speaking about tongues in a negative way. He actually embraces the gift and wishes that "all would speak in tongues …" and even says at the end of chapter 14 "do not forbid to speak in tongues …," but I digress.

CRUCIBLE

I remember reading that story *The Crucible* by Arthur Miller, but this isn't a book review on that. Where were we? Ah yes. The crucible: the "furnace of affliction"! Another truth that's not quite whole as we look into the scriptures.

Behold, I have refined you, but not as silver; I have tested you in the furnace of affliction.

Isaiah 48:10 NASB

The refining pot is for silver and the furnace for gold, But the LORD tests hearts.

Proverbs 17:3 NASB

The crucible for silver and the furnace for gold, but people are tested by their praise.

Proverbs 27:21 NIV

Are these powerful verses? Absolutely. Especially Proverbs 27! "But people are tested by their praise"! Whoa! That's what I'm talking about! These verses, however, are buffet items. Check out the nature of these three verses. Refining. Tested. Pot. Furnace. Crucible. Those all refer to what happens to silver and gold.

But God! The best two words in all of scripture. But the Lord TESTS hearts. But people are TESTED by their praise. What are you praising today? Are you paying more attention to the devil in the details than you are the Lord of the details? Is there a testing? A sanctifying work to be done in the heart of sons and daughters? Absolutely. But it's not to remove the impurity of wickedness and sin; Christ has already done that. The testing comes to reveal the purity within which has already been established for those who are in Christ. He traded us for our shame so that we could be adorned with His righteousness. It's that simple. It's a simple Gospel.

The issue many of us face is the difference of WHY is this happening instead of WHAT is happening. Asking God "why" is a pitfall for Christians, for two reasons: 1) We end up calling into question the very nature of God by 2) Focusing on the discomfort of what God has allowed to take place in my life. Talking to God about what's going on in my life is an amazing opportunity that we have as sons and daughters. When I focus on "Why God,

Why?" it's quite possible that we are taking a magnifying glass to the things I deem uncomfortable and am asking Him to remove it. This is the "crucible" theology. The "I'm just a worm who's sinned" theology. The "sinner saved by grace" theology.

By taking this point of view, even from a post-resurrection conversion, we are partnering with the belief that God is not pleased with us until we have removed every bit of impurity from our lives by enduring the pain of the furnace. CHRIST ALREADY PAID FOR IT! Why am I questioning God if He's allowed me to walk into an uncomfortable situation?

Let's ask Paul and Silas. Acts 16 gives the account where Lydia is converted, and Paul and Silas are thrown in jail. Most of us would look at this as the crucible of ministry. This is the blazing furnace that we must walk into just like Shadrach, Meshach, and Abednego. But that's just the problem. We look at their imprisonment as a test to see if they will pass. They've already passed. They're already accepted by God and loved by Him. They weren't thrown in jail as a test, but even if they were; they passed with flying colors.

About midnight Paul and Silas were praying and singing hymns to God ...."

Acts 16:25a NIV

If Proverbs 27 is any solace in the prison, it needs to be the bedrock where we lay our theology when we're between the rock and the jail cell door. Proverbs 27:21 eludes to what takes place inside a man when he is praised. A truer test cannot be found than of a man when he is praised by God, even through the encouragement of another. The same can be said for when he isn't praised. And yet, if praise is our response, no matter the circumstance, then our hearts have proven themselves pure and steadfast in the face of adversity! Praise in the prison is where the true test lies. Will we praise the Lord of heaven? Or will we bow down to the gates that bind us? Bowing down to the "crucible" before us? I wonder what the American church would look like if we recognized, as Paul and Silas did, that every prison is a circumstance, or even a chance, for the Gospel of Christ to be shared. Jail cells (e.g., work, home, friends, family, marriage, ministry, etc.) is not necessarily the crucible, but rather the place where God may have allowed you to go in order to make an impact for the Kingdom.

Do you see it? The Kingdom is all about perspective. If your perspective is inwardly focused when it comes to your circumstances, you'll see the crucible where God has set a captive audience. Whereas, if you allow your perspective to shift from inward to outward, during times of trial and persecution, you may realize that your circumstances have set you up for more miracles in Philippi; meaning your ministry won't just stay at the river tent meeting! But your praise might start shaking some jail cells so that the only option left for the jailer is to bow to the ground and, as Jack Taylor says, "get saved on accident." But as we all know, there are no accidents in the Kingdom of God.

When God keeps you out of certain districts so you can't share the good news with "that" group of people, recognize that He's up to something. If Paul and Silas would have said, "God! Why won't you let us do what we want to do?" then they would have missed Lydia and her family along with the jailer and his. When God shuts a door, begin to ask Him "what are you up to?" and allow Him to invite you into His plan; which ends up being better than my plan 1000% of the time.

SANCTI-WHAT?

Sanctification is a real term from the Bible. It's also the excuse that most "Bible scholars" use in order to say that we are still "sinners." 1 Corinthians 6:11 says, "Such were some of you, but you WERE washed, but you WERE sanctified, but you

WERE justified in the name of the Lord Jesus Christ and the Spirit of our God."

Does Jesus still need to be sanctified? No? Because He's Jesus! Then why do I, being a born-again believer in Jesus Christ, need to be sanctified any more if Christ now lives in me? The Spirit of God resides in me! The Spirit of Jesus is living through me! Why do I need to "be" sanctified if Christ has already done that great work? It sounds like we're trying to strive for our "good enough" status so that we can enter into His gates approved... but scripture actually says "Enter into His gates with thanksgiving and His courts with praise." What now?

It's quite possible that we accept a "crucible" theology so that we can continue to strive and work and plead our "goodness" before God; hoping that it's something that we do to inherit our sanctification. Our "goodness" is nothing that we attained except by the free gift of life that was offered to us by Christ Jesus. We cannot "try" to receive a gift. We either do, or we do not. There is no try! (Thanks, Yoda!) It's also quite possible that we accept a "crucible" theology so that we can continue on sinning; because we think we're "still sinners working through our salvation."

Now, do bad things happen? Absolutely. Do good Christians get diagnoses of cancer? Die in car crashes? Get divorced? Yes. Pain and brokenness are still a big part of the world and unfortunately a big part of the life of a follower of Christ. If we continue to focus on what's broken, we will continue to ask God "Why have you let me?!?" The focus of that question is more on why have "I" had to endure such pain instead of "God, what are You up to?" The latter gives Him the benefit of the doubt that He isn't finished even though it's dark out. The idea that "I'm a sinner" keeps my heart from its desire to co-labor with God.

I know what I'm asking you to do may feel like it's impossible. I have not had to bear the loss of a close family member just yet, but as I have walked with others in their grief when we begin to ask God "what are You up to" we begin to see the fullness in the midst of the brokenness. As family members unite to celebrate the loved one they've lost, we begin to see how the crucible of celebration is a much deeper and passionate flame that can forge the deepest relationships and the most whole versions of ourselves this side of heaven.

THE CRUCIBLE OF CELEBRATION

What removes pain faster than any drug? What heals our brokenness faster than any surgery? What shifts our perspective quicker than any thought? Celebration. If there's one thing you can walk away from this book with, it's the fact that God celebrates YOU. Heaven is a culture of celebration! When one that was lost is restored to the Kingdom, there's a CELEBRATION! When God is praised in heaven, He is CELEBRATED!

It's in the fires of celebration that creativity is refined in its purest form. Belief, life, and love are nurtured into roaring flames of desire through this intense Kingdom crucible. This furnace is the place where weary hearts are rekindled back into passionate wildfires! Crucibles are where precious things are made more valuable. And I'm of the belief that celebration is where God wants to reveal your true worth! And it's in this kiln that He wants to set you as His vessel!

Let's not wait till the casket is full before we start celebrating our friends and family! Let's not wait till heaven before we make that shout of glory! Let's use the time we have now to celebrate those in our lives! And watch how God can turn a prison cell into a Holy Ghost service—full of life and salvation!

CHAPTER SEVEN

DIGGING WITH DONKEYS

It is good that you are enthusiastic and passionate about spiritual gifts, especially prophecy. When someone speaks in tongues, no one understands a word he says, because he's not speaking to people, but to God—he is speaking intimate mysteries in the Spirit. But when someone prophesies, he speaks to encourage people, to build them up, and to bring them comfort. The one who speaks in tongues advances his own spiritual progress, while the one who prophesies builds up the church. I would be delighted if you all spoke in tongues, but I desire even more that you impart prophetic revelation to others. Greater gain comes through the one who prophesies than the one who speaks in tongues unless there is interpretation so that it builds up the entire church.

1 Corinthians 14:1-5 TPT

THE PROPHET

"In the beginning ... God created." Creativity was born.

"The earth was formless and void. Darkness. Spirit of God was moving ...."

"Then God said ...." The prophetic was born.

"Let there be light, AND THERE WAS LIGHT. God saw, and the light was good ...."

From the beginning of time, there has been a Prophet, speaking and imparting revelation over that which was formless, void, dark and deep. If there's anything we can surmise from a brief peek at Genesis 1, it is that when the Spirit starts to move, the prophetic gets stirred. The very Spirit of God is fueled for the opportunity to prophesy over that which isn't so, that it has the opportunity to "become." Creativity is partnered with prophecy on Day 1 of the Creation Story, and that has been God's model for Kingdom messages ever since.

Another spiritual father of mine, Bill Buckley, says it this way, "A prophetic word opens the Kingdom realm for all kinds of other supernatural possibilities." Whoa! God uses the ministry of prophecy to start stirring up the room for more. This means there's a need and a place for prophetic worship, prophetic teams and prophetic preaching in our fellowships.

Someone just said, "Whoa, whoa, whoa. Prophetic worship? Give me a break!"

Every worship song that's birthed at one time or another is a prophetic utterance. At the moment of discovery, a song that had never been sung before rings out into the atmosphere and something with each individual within earshot shifts. Yes! Every songwriter, author, and poet are prophets! And they didn't even know it!

Then comes the moment where the song is led for the first time in a corporate setting. Usually, it's about two or three songs into the worship set, and then a new guitar/piano riff takes off, and something begins to stir. Unfamiliar lyrics captivate and open the eyes of all in the room to read what they're hearing. Without knowing it, they instinctively begin singing along with the new tune, drawn in by what it's speaking in that space and time. Sometime later, when the service is over, everyone is talking about that "new song." Little did they know that it was the creativity, spontaneity, and ability to prophesy newness that stirred hearts to awaken. Too many leaders today discourage the use of new songs because of their repetition or style but wonder why their worship atmosphere seems to be lacking.

Now, before we move on it should be said: not every new song is a prophetic song, and not every old song is a dead song. Sometimes the Lord lays an old song on your heart in the middle of worship, this is a prophetic moment for the people of God to find breakthrough. Let's not limit the prophetic to what is "new" but allow permission for what is "God's". There are beautiful times where a new song is written in worship, there's also times where an old chorus is the linchpin for the more!

Revelation 4:8 says, "Each of the four living creatures had six wings, full of eyes all around and under their wings. They worshiped without ceasing, day and night, singing, 'Holy, holy, holy is the Lord God, the Almighty! The Was, the Is, and the Coming!'" There is repetition in the presence of God in heaven. It may be time we incorporate repetition in our worship, in the presence, before the Lord God, "The Almighty!"

Prophetic worship is simply taking risks hearing from God and singing what needs to be sung so that freedom can reign. Just like riding a bike takes practice, so does trying anything new. I remember a few years ago I finally tried to Rip Stick—ate it immediately. For those of you who only know about skateboards, a Rip Stick is a board with two independent wheels, that you have to use your own momentum to propel the board forward.

It was then that I thought about retiring from the wild and exciting world of Rip Sticking. But over the next week, I tried to ride it for at least five minutes every day. By the end of the week, I was wheeling through the halls of my church like a concrete surfer. Sometime later someone asked where I learned to ride so well, and the realization hit me, "I couldn't do this a few weeks ago ... but now it's as if I've always known how to ride. I wonder what else I can do that I've written off?" We can achieve anything we put our mind to.

If we set out to have a stunning worship service with limited mistakes and flawless transitions, you know what we'll end up with? A stunning worship service with limited mistakes (hopefully) and flawless transitions. But if we run after what we think God is doing in that place, at that moment, and practice risking it for the sake of releasing something over our land/people, guess what we'll end up with? An atmosphere where we don't know when the transition comes, but we see tears in the eyes and people getting right with each other because what we released that morning was permission. Permission to step out of the box and engage a God who's inviting us into the more. It's super messy. But the risk is so worth it.

The Passion Translation puts it this way, in Psalm 62:2 (Emphasis added):

> *He alone is my safe place; his wrap-around presence always protects me. For he is my champion defender; **there's no risk of failure with God**. So why would I let worry paralyze me, even when troubles multiply around me?*

DIGGING FOR GOLD

Let's jump back into 1 Corinthians 14. But before we do I think it's worth saying, prophecy in the Old Testament was not necessarily the "turn or burn" plotline that many have adopted as the "true" way to give a Word from the Lord. I wish we could go there, but for time's sake, think about it this way: If we read where God spoke through the OT prophets and imagine He (as Leonard Ravenhill would say) had a tear in His eye for the people who had turned away from Him, we might look at God as a Father who is heartbroken over His children instead of a vindictive dictator who's out for vengeance.

You know what, let's go there; if only for a moment. Ezekiel is a book of the Bible that so many look to and say that God is just downright finished with His people, yet why does He have this prophet standing on a wall, as a watchman, to warn the people? A good prophet will warn the people. And a warning isn't condemnation. It's a warning. Period. This is God's invitation for those who are warned to take heed and turn. Sounds kind of like turn or burn, right? It is. But hear the heart behind it and not the voice of your grandpa's preacher.

There are consequences to not obeying the rules. While under the rules we enjoy the boundaries and protections they offer. But once outside the letter of the law, we complain and backbite the Lord and say "what an unfair God we serve." Thus, our great need for Jesus to come and die is pivotal, so that the law would be completed and no longer useful for those who are now in Christ. Now we have a new standard for prophecy, and it comes from 1 Corinthians.

1 Corinthians 14:3 says, "But when someone prophesies, he speaks to encourage people, to build them up, and to bring them comfort." Man, I guess Paul forgot to add in there, "and to smite the jaw of the wicked, to speak down to the sinner, and to rip apart the pastor of other fellowships because they're wrong!" Oh, and what about, "continue to gossip about any and every individual that we have a problem with and disguise it as prayer."

Nope. Paul understands that he was there to share the tone and character of Christ. He, himself, had a radical transformation with Jesus where the Savior of the world spoke to him, blinded him and gave him specific instructions. Then Jesus has an in-depth conversation with Ananias about restoring Saul.

Hebrews 9:27-28 (NASB) says, "And inasmuch as it is appointed for men to die once and after this comes judgment, so Christ also, having been offered once to bear the sins of many, will appear a second time for salvation **without reference to sin**, to those who eagerly await Him." If we find ourselves reading the Word and seeing God angry, try reading it as if God has a smile on His face. Too often we add our own filtered version of God to the Bible.

Back to 1 Corinthians 14. If our purpose in prophesying is to extract the precious from those we're speaking to, we will fulfill the command to "encourage people, build them up, and bring them comfort." In our community, we call this "Digging for Gold." We also call it "finding the gold," "calling out the gold," or what most know as "prophesying." Imagine with me, for a moment, that every single son and daughter of the Most-High God has a huge, I mean I'm talking huge, piece of gold right in the center of their chest. What would you do? Point it out, right?

Well, what if I were to tell you, that this piece of gold is covered up with mud and muck and sewage ... what would you do then? Getting into other people's mess isn't exactly what we signed up for when we stepped up into this Christian life, is it? I love what Teo Van Der Welle says, "Discipleship should look less like trash collecting, and more like pearl diving."

"Prophecy is the great equalizer. I can walk into a house of poverty or a king's palace and change the whole atmosphere with a prophetic word" (Bill Buckley).

The best way to be a "Gold-Digger" is first to spend time refining the gold from God's heart so that we can know what we're looking for in the hearts of others. A number of times in Scripture a man has a chance to encounter God on His throne in the realm of Heaven. While seated on this throne there is color and sound, and thickness; yet Ezekiel and John specifically speak about the colors emanating from the throne. Ezekiel says in 1:27, "Then I noticed from the appearance of His loins and upward something like *glowing metal that looked like fire* all around within it ...." The "metal that looked like fire" is the amber stone and in some stones, it looks like there are tongues of fire. Amber is a fossilized resin, meaning that it comes from something living (Hmm) and in the recollection of Ezekiel is bright and powerful.

This is conjecture at best but indulge me for a moment. When the prophet looked on Him who is, he saw fire in His chest. Is it any coincidence that when the Spirit of God begins to move, at least in my life, I begin to feel a burning in my chest? Ironically, there were tongues of fire being dispersed in Acts 2! Regardless of irrefutable facts, I am of the belief that God's heart is made of fiery gold, and our job as adopted sons and daughters is to excavate and mine for the gold He's placed in the hearts of those around us. If we choose to accept this view of a Kingdom calling, we will no longer be terrified to reach out to our families, coworkers or even strangers; because we're just looking for Him in their story. Go for the gold, and

You'll find Him and them in the process. We are all created in God's image, so there's a bit of God's gold in every man, woman, and child on the planet!

DONKEYS

As some of you know, there is a direct correlation between donkeys and prophets in the Bible. For those of you who didn't know that, or if you were about to pull out your Bible app to fact check, take a look at Numbers 22. I'll give you a quick recap. A dude named Balak is looking for Balaam to be a prophet and prophesy against the people of Israel. God says no. Balaam says no. Balak asks again. God says, "OK, but do only what I tell you." The prophet saddles up his donkey and decides to go. God gets mad and sets an angel in Balaam's way.

> *When the donkey saw the angel of the Lord standing in the road with a drawn sword in his hand, it turned off the road into a field. Balaam beat it to get it back on the road. Then the angel of the Lord stood in a narrow path through the vineyards, with walls on both sides. When the donkey saw the angel of the Lord, it pressed close to the wall, crushing Balaam's foot against it. So, he beat the donkey again. Then the angel of the Lord moved on ahead and stood in a narrow place where there was no room to turn, either to the right or to the left. When the donkey saw the angel of the Lord, it lay down under Balaam, and he was angry and beat it with his staff. Then the Lord opened the donkey's mouth, and it said to Balaam, "What have I done to you to make you beat me these three times?"*
>
> Numbers 22:23-28 NIV

You might be prophetic, but when you need a donkey to speak up, it might be high time to realize who the real "Jack" is. This man beat his donkey! Why? Because it didn't do what he deemed appropriate? Let me say this. Too often in the American church today, we beat those who don't follow our way of "right." What if God has set an angel in front of them and they are acting on our behalf to save us from our own crash course with destruction? Here we intersect with what we've always believed and what God may be trying to reveal to us. Are we the only instrument of God's purposes? Or is God trying to speak through a donkey?

Balaam finally gets his donkey under "control," and they continue. This time the beast runs its masters foot into the wall. Another beating. How many times do we need to be detoured before we'll recognize the signs?

A third time. A third beating. But this time the donkey just lays down. Have we beaten the life out of those who God is using to protect us? I think it's hilarious that God told Balaam not to go in the first place because he would be prophesying against Joshua and all of Israel! Imagine being the guy to get called for that job? Not only did he turn it down, by God's warning, but when they came back he didn't even consult God about it, then the Lord had to come to him. How often do we leave God out of our lives, and process for ourselves?

Well, God had to come to Balaam, and then Balaam's donkey had to speak in order to get this man's attention. And the story goes on. The Angel of the Lord eventually opens Balaam's eyes, and he finally realizes that the beast he wished he could kill just saved his life. Long story short, it was a reminder that Balaam needed to speak only what the Lord spoke and sometimes God wants to use your circumstances to do it. Read the rest of Chapters 22-25. Balaam only had three chances to avoid the Angel of the Lord, while Balak asks time and time again to hear from the prophet only what he wanted to hear. Are you looking for someone to tickle your ears? Or are you looking for what God is speaking?

God used a prophet (a donkey) to get a prophet's (Balaam's) attention. And it got me wondering. For a short time, I was working in landscaping here in Starkville, MS. I drove all around this small college town, out into the country and all over. On my route, I started to notice something peculiar in the herds as I passed ranches and farms. In the middle of all of these cows, sheep, and goats there would be a donkey. Now, for those of you who don't know, I grew up in Virginia Beach, VA (757); we didn't have sheep and goats and donkeys. I had to look this up.

An article in *Modern Farmer* written by Tyler Leblanc said: "Although often portrayed as moody and difficult to work with, donkeys, if trained right, can be loyal and effective farm hands …" and it went on to say, that instead of using dogs, who need to be fed differently from sheep, donkeys can graze with the herd and are relatively low maintenance. It went on to say that young donkeys are particularly loud and need to be introduced to skittish sheep inside the safety of a pen, for a time, to acclimate the sheep to the obnoxious donkey. Once acclimated, the herd will adopt the donkey as their own, and the donkey will adopt the territory as its own. Being quite social, the donkey will graze and roam with the herd until it senses a threat.

Now a donkey can't take on much more than a single attacker at a time, however, they are a stubborn bunch. First, they'll cry out if their eyes or ears have picked something up; this is a warning for their herd that something's going on. Next, if the predator gets close enough, it will charge after it, hoping to spook intruders from its land. If none of this works, donkeys will bite and kick and thrash about like a wild thing until either the intruder is gone or its life is spent.

Hopefully, at this point, you've recognized that I'm no longer talking about donkeys.

THE PROPHETIC

There are four different lists of spiritual gifts in the new testament. Romans 12 has a list of seven Motivational gifts. The seven Motivational Gifts are:

1) Prophecy
2) Serving
3) Teaching
4) Exhorting
5) Giving
6) Organizing
7) Mercy

Notice #1. Prophecy. A person who is prophetically motivated is driven by a sense of right and wrong, black and white, good and evil. They are stereotypically blunt, strong-willed and reminiscent of a "Jack." For years churches have been driving away such people because they tend to be loud, obnoxious and are always shouting of an attack and impending doom. Shepherds, who are concerned about the sheep, see the "donkeys" driving away the "herd" and instinctively remove the sore thumb. The problem is when you remove the donkey you end up leaving your sheep unattended and unprotected. You also scar the donkey and ensure a future of broken relationships and distance from community.

Prophets are donkeys. Often considered moody and difficult to work with, but if trained properly, can be loyal and effective. When the enemy comes as a coyote to steal one of the precious lambs, the donkey will cry, charge and fight to the death (if necessary) in order to protect that which dwells in his territory. The problem is, donkeys have very large ears and very wide eyes; and from a distance, it can look like a donkey, who is punching the ground, has lost its mind. Its hooves are pounding, it's voice shrieking, and all we can think is "please, someone put that poor beast out of its misery." However, no one seems to suspect the serpent in the grass. No one suspects that danger is not around the corner, but it's in the pasture—no one except the donkey.

I have such a motivation. I am justice oriented. Repentance is my lifeblood. Protection is my cause. I have been the squeaky wheel for years, not understanding that what I was seeing, hearing, feeling and sensing was a gift from God to protect the pasture I was placed in. The leaders I served under didn't know what to do with me, cause I'm the loud donkey who's making a big deal out of everything. Young donkeys must be trained and introduced to a herd at a young age in order to acclimate well with those who are more skittish. But if we in the church, only want our quiet fields with tithing balls of wool, we will drive out those God has sent to warn us and leave ourselves exposed and defenseless.

Let me talk to the "sheep" for a minute. Church, it's time to embrace the fullness of the body. Our communities should look less like a cookie cutter bake sale, and more like a potluck: messy and family style. It's time we round out the field in our ministries and our communities. Begin to highlight the donkeys. Spend time with them. Nurture them. Also listen to them. To you, they may be going berserk for no good reason, but they also might be detecting the slithering snakes that are hidden in the tall grasses.

"Donkeys," you're not off the hook either. Volume is not a precursor of correctness. The sheep are freaked out by the way we look, the way we talk and the way we, well, just the way we are. It is time the prophets stopped speaking the truth without love and burning every bridge they cross. Guess what? If we end up standing in a field alone, and one day we look up and there's no one to talk to, it might be high time to figure out how to graze and gaze. What do I mean by that? If we're in a new season and in a new herd, God may be inviting us into a season of silence, even when we feel like raising the alarm. We need to keep our eyes and ears open! And our head down! Nibble on some grass. We need to learn what our community is learning and become adaptable to the grazing patterns that they find comfortable. And just chill out. A day will come when the serpents slither in, and the coyotes try to sneak in for a meal. On that day, I give us permission to "Jack" some demons up. But until then, we must learn how to be one of the herd.

Let's turn now to the shepherd. Pastor. Remember, the donkey's that God has brought into our life might turn abruptly into the adjacent field. Will we follow their prompting or beat them like Balaam? What happens when our foot gets smashed because the prophet in our midst got us jammed in between a rock and a hard place? Will we check on them or beat them like Balaam? And even when there's no place to turn and they see the Angel of the Lord set to strike you down, will we beat them again when they decide to lay down beneath us? Cause I'm telling you from experience, any prophet that lays down to accept the fate of your malice is really telling you, "You can beat me all you want, but I would rather die than lead you to your own death." A donkey is a key commodity in a Kingdom Family. They might need a little more love and a little more attention than the rest, but the dividends much outweigh the means.

This is not a call to sell it all, purchase some land and find a few donkeys. This is a prophet's plea to cultivate community in such a way that we end up accepting one another, instead of looking for mirror images of ourselves. We are in need of others who don't think like us, act like us or sound like us to help round out the herd, so to speak, in order to look and act more like Jesus. He was able to be every single one of those Motivational Gifts, each in their own way and time. By embracing the fullness of the body of Christ, we can come to accept differing styles and opinions on open handed issues because we are all in process. Just realize that when the donkeys start crying that it might be an invitation from God to slow down, seek Him and alter our course.

CHAPTER EIGHT

DEFENDING THE UNOFFENDED

THUNDER

Remember those lads in *Braveheart* talking about William Wallace? How he was seven feet tall and all that? To which he (Mel Gibson) replies in his Australian/American/Scottish brogue, "Yes, I've heard. Kills men by the hundreds. And if *he* were here, he'd consume the English with fireballs from his eyes, and bolts of lightning from his arse" (*Braveheart* movie).

Well, there's a bit of scripture that sounds not too unlike this excerpt from the film. The "Sons of Thunder" from Luke 9! Well, they were affectionately referred to as "Sons of Thunder" in Mark 3, but it's the same story. I just love Luke! Anyway; back to Luke 9. In verse 49, John says, "Master, we saw someone casting out demons in Your name; and we tried to prevent him because he does not follow along with us." Jesus replied, "Do not hinder him; for he who is not against you is for you."

Just a few verses later James and John are ready to bring down the thunder!

Thunder, feel the thunder (clap, clap, clap)
Lightning and the Thunder
(Imagine Dragons, *Thunder*)

A village doesn't receive Jesus and the Thunder Boys pipe up, "Lord, do You want us to command fire to come down from heaven and consume them?" Read that again with a Scottish accent! Trust me; it's worth it!

Jesus replies and rebukes them saying, "You do not know what kind of spirit you are of; for the Son of Man did not come to destroy men's lives but to save them." I've always heard it's better to have to slow someone down rather than have to speed them up, but Jesus drops a bit of thunder on these boys and I'm not so sure calling down the fire is exactly the kind of thing that advances the Kingdom. But how often do we end up trying to "prevent" someone from operating in Kingdom work? And how often do we call down "fire" upon our brothers and sisters in Christ all because we don't agree with their theology?

Thunder, feel the thunder (clap, clap, clap)
Lightning and the Thunder
(Imagine Dragons, *Thunder)*

CUSS WORDS

Here it is. You're going to make me cuss: Vindication! Justification! There I go! Sweetmeat pies!

"But Caleb … Isn't Justification what Jesus did in order to trade in our sins for Righteousness?"

Why yes, that is absolutely correct. However, I look at justification as a cuss word because in the church today we use it as a means to say anything we want about anyone—all in the name of justifying ourselves. We also hope to vindicate our case by coming up with facts and figures that we found on the Internet of which we all know to be the bedrock of all truth and justice. Who cares if we smear someone's name on social "MEdia" as long as *I* look like *I'm* right?

"Well! They should have thought about that before they decided to go off the deep end with what they believe!" we might say to ourselves.

If we have ever found ourselves attacking a fellow Christian, or even a group of non-Christians for that matter, we may be a little more "child of thunder" than we think. Refer back to Luke 9:55-56. Take a good, long, look at the first few words there! Then let it sink in real deep as you read the rest of the verses.

Jesus came to SAVE! Not destroy! Yet everywhere we look these days someone is using their social "MEdia" platform to criticize and destroy another God-created human being, all in the name of vindication and justification.

WHO'S OFFENDED?

We may think to ourselves, "But they're making God look bad! We have to say something in order to correct their wrong theology/practice/teaching!"

I hear this argument all the time. I actually stood on that platform for a huge majority of my life, fighting to vindicate God because I thought He was clearly upset and offended by those preaching the word incorrectly! Just like Peter, I had to rebuke the "sons of thunder"! Wait, Peter didn't rebuke them? Did Jesus? Wait! What are we supposed to do when someone doesn't represent Christ well?

LET JESUS HANDLE IT!

"But what if God put us in their path to correct it?"

LET JESUS HANDLE IT!

"But what if they don't understand the Greek and Hebrew text?"

Ας το χειριστεί ο Ιησούς! זת YESUS לפטל הז!

"But what if they don't understand how wrong they are?"

LET JESUS HANDLE IT!

The funny thing is we're not actually defending God; we're actually trying to defend ourselves. #SayWhat Anytime we get on our social "MEdia" soapbox in order to run someone down for believing or teaching the wrong thing, it's usually from the position of explaining our own "correct" beliefs, disguised in the name of God's beliefs. The question still remains, "Who's offended?" Before running into the battle of theological correctness, hoping we can defend God almighty, it might be a good idea to check and see if the twinge we're feeling is something that's not lining up with scripture versus something not lining up with what we've found in scripture. One is God's Word; the other is our interpretation of God's Word.

DEFENDING THE UNDEFENDED

Remember the story of the woman caught in adultery? If not, go check it out. John 8.

As the story goes, Jesus is teaching in the temple when the religious elite show up with a woman they've "caught" in adultery. They bring her before Jesus and try to trap him. If Jesus doesn't agree with the law of Moses, then they can accuse Him (kind of like they're accusing her) of wrongdoing and probably try to stone him too. If Jesus does agree with the law of Moses, then He is condoning them to stone her, which would probably lead Him to being stoned too.

What to do? What to do?

What would you do? Back in my day, which wasn't so long ago, I'd probably look for some eloquent way to debate these bozos until they were thoroughly stumped and had to walk away licking their wounds. Or I'd be pummeled to death by rocks and having the dogs lick my wounds instead. It's a tricky situation because, on the one hand, you have a group of religious leaders who are dead to rights on their beliefs. They are well within their means, based on the law, to stone this chick and call it a day. On the other hand, you have this woman who has been publicly disgraced and standing trial in the middle of the temple with men all around her (perhaps even men that have slept with her themselves, or even snuck a peek at her standing there). She's immersed in a society that doesn't value her, so at this point in life, she probably doesn't feel very valuable. You also have this prophet, this Messiah, named Jesus who is caught in between the two. What would you do?

Jesus didn't condemn the Pharisees! He simply said, in John 8:7, "He who is without sin among you, let him be the FIRST to throw a stone at her." Be the FIRST! Not the only! But the first! The first? "Yo, Jesus! You just signed her death certificate!" Or so it would seem. Jesus is actually protecting this particular group of men by giving them a way out. Almost restating what He dropped in Matthew 7 where He says "Do not judge or else, you'll be judged" (COR: Caleb's Own Recollection). He doesn't say to them, "Yo! You all have sinned and fallen short of the glory of God! Take a seat!" He actually joins in and says, "Go for it! Oh yeah, but before you do, make sure the best of you goes first! We wouldn't want them, who are justified, to miss out."

They came at Him with words written in stone, by the finger of the Almighty. What they didn't know is that the Almighty was kneeling in the flesh before them, demonstrating a new law—one written by His own finger in the dust. He was demonstrating hearts of stone turning to hearts of flesh. He was showing the prophetic picture of getting a new heart.

As you read this are you angry? Or are you refreshed? If anger is being birthed, it's quite possible that your heart of stone is so rigid and set in its ways that it's impossible to see life any differently than how you've written it on your own *stony* heart. If you're refreshed, then it's quite possible that Jesus has the final say of what is and what isn't in your life and that your heart is a little dustier than others. Meaning: when Jesus decides to reveal something new to you, He's able to wipe away what was and take His finger and write on your heart. This Christian walk has the opportunity to be filled with new revelations instead of set expectations. The more times God writes on what was my heart of stone, the more flecks of dust appear; soon giving way to just a dusty heart.

If we feel the need to vindicate God, the law, the Bible or Jesus; we must make sure we're not just defending the words on a page (or on a stone for that matter) and remember to reflect the heart and nature of the One we're so desperately trying to defend.

Let's get back to John 8.

Jesus didn't condemn the woman. I know you've heard it before but think about it. If there was anyone in the room who had the right to strike that woman down it was Jesus. But the Prince of Peace is not concerned with ridding the world of the offensive but defending the undefended.

You see, the Pharisee's sense of right didn't account for what was wrong. Or even what was right for her. This is a case where being right can be so terribly wrong. Which is better? Am I defending myself? Or defending another? Making sure I'm right? Or helping another to be seen as right? Jesus stands and looks the woman in the eye and says, "I do not condemn you either."

Isaiah 33:22 says, "For the LORD is our judge, The LORD is our lawgiver, The LORD is our king; He will save us."

DEFENDING THE UNOFFENDED

In our desperate plea to be seen, recognized and validated we hope to defend the One who isn't offended. The religious elite came to Jesus thinking that He'd be horrified at this woman's actions and cast a stone with them; this just wasn't the case.

How often do we join the accuser in condemning God's sons and daughters with well-meaning rhetoric and partially well crafted theology? To have a Biblical stance that says, "We can treat others as lesser than us because they lack the knowledge we have," is a sad stance, indeed. Instead, we can stand up like Jesus did and gently draw people to the conclusion that it might not be the best course of action; leaving that up to them.

Our job is not to defend the scriptures, but to present them to those we come into contact with. Our work is to encourage those around us with the teachings of God in order to build them up and strengthen faith. But in order to do so, we first have to recognize any traces of offense from our own lives so that we can begin to walk in the purity of the scriptures with the Lord, working on voiding all malice and anger from misinterpretation and lack of experience.

If Jesus says that we will perform more miracles than He did, I have to believe Him.

If Jesus says we are to proclaim the Kingdom, cast out demons, heal the sick and cure disease, I have to believe Him.

The next time someone lights up the news feed on social "Media" with something that offends you, ask yourself this question, "What can I do to stand with them like Jesus?"

And when someone decides to teach something at church that goes against everything you've ever been taught, ask yourself, "What can I do to stand with them like Jesus?"

Maybe this week you and someone in your family will get into an argument about something silly, it's times like that to ask yourself, "What can I do to stand with them like Jesus?"

Jesus stood with the Pharisee and the woman. Will you?

CHAPTER NINE

LEADERSHEEP

SHEEP?

During my years at Liberty University, I spent my summer months working at a camp called Triple R Ranch. Some of my favorite memories stem back to those days of camp, friends, and ministry; but ironically enough, the lesson that lodged itself deep into my soul was through Mary and Martha. Oh, to be clear Mary and Martha weren't the cute counselors that summer, they were our Camp Director's sheep.

Betty, our Camp Director, was fascinated by these animals; something I would come to acquire later on in life. In the meantime, I just thought they were dumb. They'd get stuck, lost, run away, spooked, and wouldn't respond to anyone at camp—anyone except Betty. She'd sit back and watch. We'd call the sheep. We'd try to entice them with food and water. We even tried to tie a leash to them to make them follow us—nothing. All of a sudden, with her head held high, Betty would step out and call, "Mary! Martha!" and from out of nowhere these two lumbering puffs of wool would come bounding across the field to their master. We all sat there with our jaws hanging wide open as Betty ruffled her feathers and grinned like a peahen.

I remember one time the sheep got loose and had run away. For days Betty would walk the property calling her babies. We thought we'd lost them. An ingenious young rascal at camp decided to play her voice over a portable sound system to see if it would help carry Betty's voice through the woodlands of the Dismal Swamp. It worked, and Mary and Martha came running home; and thus, the sheep pen under the BMX deck was born.

BUT WHY SHEEP?

Here's the deal about sheep. They're not very bright. If a gust of wind blows the wrong direction, sheep will scatter. If another sheep bleats too loud, sheep will scatter. If a fly buzzes around a sheep's head, it will scatter. If it's hungry, it will scatter. If it's too hot, it will scatter. If it's too cold, sheep will scatter. It it's sick, sheep with scatter. If there are wolves, it will scatter. If the shepherds not paying attention, they will scatter. If there's a storm, sheep will scatter. You can't reason with them. They're not terribly easy to lead, especially if the shepherd is not overly invested into their well-being. God tells that to Ezekiel in chapter 34. Check it out.

Here's the thing, though. Sheep recognize their shepherd's voice. In order to recognize it though, sheep have to be in constant contact and relationship with their shepherd. This is why Jesus says in John 10:1-5 (NASB),

> *Truly, truly, I say to you, he who does not enter by the door into the fold of the sheep, but climbs up some other way, he is a thief and a robber. But he who enters by the door is a shepherd of the sheep. To him, the doorkeeper opens, and the sheep hear his voice, and he calls his own sheep by name and leads them out. When he puts forth all his own, he goes ahead of them, and the sheep follow him because they know his voice. A stranger they simply will not follow, but will flee from him, because they do not know the voice of strangers.*

After reading this, I realized why Mary and Martha wouldn't "hither" to my call. I was a stranger to them. They only knew and followed the voice of the one they *knew*. Just like us, when we come into contact with the *true* Shepherd of our souls, we respond to His voice. I wonder if the reason some of our churches aren't seeing salvations and consistency in attendance is because we've traded in His voice for our own?

There's another reason sheep are scattered, that I didn't mention earlier, and that's due to a thief. He doesn't enter through the door/gate but comes to steal, kill and destroy. A lack of "bah's" in the pews is not always a sign of poor leadership; it can be a sign of crafty thieves. If you remember back to the "Devil in the Details," the enemy is constantly trying to desecrate God's voice so that he can scatter yours. The enemy will come in and cause division in the "fold" so that the shepherd can't lead. The storms come, and the sheep are swept away in the torrent of waters through a dry and thirsty land.

HOW TO SHEEP?

Before we get further into the idea of "leadersheep," let's take a look at the responsibilities of a shepherd in Biblical times. You might be saying, "Whoa, whoa. I don't know anything about sheep; nor do I care." (Pat yourself on the back if you said "nor"). In the American church, the idea of shepherds and sheep is lost on those who didn't grow up on a farm (or working at summer camp with sheep). We could talk about coaching, teaching, leading, recruiting, etc., and I'd have a much easier time relating to the culture. But my job isn't to relate you back to the culture you're in, my hope is to relate you to the culture of heaven. Heaven is a community that likes to talk about shepherding and sheep.

Let's take a look at Psalm 23. You guessed it. The "Lord is my SHEPHERD" chapter. For the sake of relativity, we'll take a look at this passage in The Passion Translation.

1. The Lord is my best friend and my shepherd. I always have more than enough.

2. He offers a resting place for me in His luxurious love. His tracks take me to an oasis of peace and the quiet brooks of bliss.

3. That's where He restores and revives my life. He opens before me pathways to God's pleasure and leads me along in His footsteps of righteousness so that I can bring honor to His name.

4. Lord, even when your path takes me through the valley of deepest darkness, fear will never conquer me, for you already have! You remain close to me and lead me through it all the way. Your authority is my strength and my peace. The comfort of your love takes away my fear. I'll never be lonely, for you are near.

5. You become my delicious feast even when my enemies dare to fight. You anoint me with the fragrance of your Holy Spirit; You give me all I can drink of You until my heart overflows.

6. So why would I fear the future? For Your goodness and love pursue me all the days of my life. Then afterward, when my life is through, I'll return to Your glorious presence to be forever with You!

Great! Sheep! Right? That's what most American Christians end up saying after reading passages like these. But let's take a look at what's actually taking place.

1. The sheep are taken care of and provided for.

2. There are designated places of rest and this shepherd knows how to find pools of fresh, still waters. To understand this concept, we have to understand the location. Shepherds in the arid plains of Israel knew when a storm came through that the hardened ground would repel the waters, causing flash floods to take place instantaneously. Psalm 32 (NASB) speaks, "Surely in a flood of great waters they will not reach him. You are my hiding place; You preserve me from

trouble; You surround me with songs of deliverance." From the perspective of Psalm 32, a good shepherd knows how to rescue his sheep in a "flood of great waters" by singing to them over the rain, thunder, and lightning. He takes them to a high place, to let the waters pass, and here lies the craftiness of shepherds. Because the ground is so hard and refuses to accept the waters, he needs to know where to go in order to find pools of fresh water where his sheep can drink from. A few days from now the stagnant waters will either be riddled with bacteria or dried up by the sun.

3. A good shepherd knows how to take care of his sheep in such a way that he revives them and restores them back to health. He then leads them on paths that are good for them to walk so they won't be hurt.

4. Let's take a look at the beginning of verse 5 to understand this verse. The NASB says "You prepare a table before me…" This is a landscape thought. A table is an elevated place where shepherds would take their sheep to graze. He would take them from one "table" to another by going through the valley. Here the shepherd is leading his sheep through a darkened place, somewhere he's already been, so he is able lead them. His rod and his staff are his authority which he uses to comfort and nudge in the right direction. His voice and his implements are used in love to direct their steps.

5. A shepherd would need to cross down through the valley himself to go prepare the next "table" for his sheep. Meaning he would clear the field of any poisonous plants, predators or fill in any holes where his sheep might break a leg. To keep the sheep nearby, he anoints their heads with oil so that flies don't annoy the sheep and drive them away. Because of this great care, their cup overflows.

6. To live a life such as this with a shepherd watching over them, these sheep are well taken care of, and they are walking in the fullness that He brings.

CLAWS OR HOOVES

There are two kinds of shepherds today:

1. Wolf-Focused
2. Sheep-Focused

Wolf-focused shepherds find it their duty to go looking for the wolves who may be infiltrating our sheep pens. The problem with this approach is that the shepherd stops listening to the sheep and starts listening for wolves. Leaders with an emphasis on the enemy will start checking every sheep to make sure there are no claws under that wool. Unfortunately, this can lead to backbiting, clawing one another and driving the sheep away. We may believe we're acting like sheepdogs to help the Shepherd, but in order to go against God's chosen is to go against God Himself.

Sheep-focused shepherds focus on sheep. This means they don't go looking for wolves, but when the wolves come (and they will), they will drive them away because they care about the sheep. We fight for what we care about. If you care about sheep, we will fight for their safety, security, welfare, healing, food, water and everything else they need.

Being a shepherd can't just be focused on keeping away the wolves but keeping the sheep safe. Watching for wolves is one aspect of shepherding, but it's not the only job requirement. The problem is: when we spend enough time thinking like a wolf, in order to catch a wolf, we might find ourself acting like a wolf. In order to be a good shepherd, we have to think like a shepherd who cares about sheep. If we think about sheep in order to protect sheep, we might find ourselves becoming a good shepherd.

NOT THE SHEEP!

It's amazing to look at scripture through the eyes of a shepherd. Their role for the sheep is to do all things because the sheep are incapable of doing anything. We as "sheep" are in great need of "shepherds"who can lead us to His best for us. Wait! Are we sheep and shepherds? Or are we just sheep? Somewhere along the way we've accepted the fact that we are all just dumb as sheep. We are not dumb sheep. We are sons and daughters and have been given leaders so that we won't be "like" sheep without a shepherd.

The Word says it plainly in Matthew 9:36 (NASB), "Seeing the people, He felt compassion for them because they were distressed and dispirited *like* sheep without a shepherd" (emphasis added).

God isn't a goat or a sheep, is He? No! He's our Father. If we are His sons, made in His image, our job is to work in the family business. We are to pick up our staffs and our rods and be shepherds (of sorts). If people aren't sheep, who are we to shepherd? We are to lead those God has entrusted us with, as if they were *like* sheep. To heal up the broken, to find the lost and to drive out predators. It seems that the emphasis in the church today is that "We are the leaders! You are the followers! Because you're a sheep, you must be dumb and in need of me!"This is not leadership. This is power consumption.

People aren't sheep when they're lost and then become shepherds when they're found. We are *like* lost sheep who need to be found but check out Luke 15. The first story is of a shepherd who lost one sheep; the second of a woman who lost one coin. The third story is about a father who lost a son. Jesus spoke in these parables to bring the people in. "Who here has lost a sheep?" It's my guess that every hand went sky high, "Oh yeah! Lost one this morning! Had to go down to little Lucy's favorite spot to get her back!"

Jesus, having already set the hook, now goes in after their heart. "Who of you have lost a coin?" Because they raise sheep and sell them, their purse would have been full from their trade. I bet a number of hands went up, saying, "Oh man! That happened to me a while back. It's not as often as Lucy runs away. But every once in a while, we lose some money. I've got to provide for my family somehow."

Now, having reeled them in, Jesus says, "How many of you have lost a son?" I expect a dull silence hung on the crowd at that point. Probably some angry parents gritted their jaws and siblings tightened their fists. The scalpel had done its work. They cared for their sheep. They cared for their coins. But how many of them really cared about their sons? About their brothers? About their fathers? This was the whole point of the sheep story. Jesus used what they knew in order to enter into their hearts.

He begins to weave a tale of a selfish son. Maybe some of those in the crowd had acted like him? Maybe others had children standing there with them who they were concerned about?

The son loses it all. Maybe there were a few in financial crisis who didn't know who to turn to?

He decides to go back home. How many of them are now contemplating heading back to their families? How many of them are now hoping for their lost ones to come back home? For those who are picking up the true intent of this message maybe they are starting to think about their heavenly Father, whom Jesus has been speaking about this whole time?

When he gets close, the Father runs to him. Tears begin to stream down some of the flushed faces of the crowd. Maybe their fathers had rejected them when they came back? Or worse, because of their custom they rejected their sons when they decided to return? Regardless, Jesus didn't need to explain this particular parable. The hammer fell, and hearts that were hardened were finally softened. The whole intention of the message was family. The whole intention of this story was love. The whole intention of this parable is that when a son comes home, we need to treat him better than we do the sheep that we've found. One lost sheep out of a hundred is important. One coin out of ten is precious, but one son, regardless of how many, is irreplaceable.

The crowd is saturated with the love of God. Then sneaky Jesus takes it a step further. This isn't a parable about one lost son; there's actually two lost sons. He recognizes the religious elite hanging out on the fringe of the crowd and says, "How many of you are a brother to one such as this?"

LEADERSHEEP!

Hopefully, by now, you've recognized that the Bible's concern for sheep is less about woolly bleaters and more about having a mindset of caring for people. Leadership should run through the belief system of Leading Sheep, thus "Leadersheep." It all comes back to John 21. You knew we had to go there.

Jesus has resurrected! Peter's back in his boat. After a sweet seaside breakfast and much conversation, Jesus leans over and asks Peter three times if he loves Him and three times Peter says, "Yes I love you." Jesus then replies, "Tend My lambs. Shepherd My sheep. Tend My sheep." There's more to it than that, but the point I'm trying to make here is this: Jesus isn't talking about sheep. The Lord of all creation sums up in a simple phrase what takes some a lifetime to understand. When Jesus says, "Tend My lambs." He's not just saying "give up the oar for a staff." He's giving Peter a mandate—a heaven sized mandate at that.

Like we saw in Psalm 23, there are a variety of ways in order to take care of the fuzzy bottom bleaters. The following is an example of some proverbial tasks of a shepherd:

1. Leading
2. Feeding
3. Anointing
4. Healing
5. Protecting
6. Securing
7. Finding

By a simple turn of phrase, Jesus tells Peter to do all these things, and more, in order to take care of the people God has trusted him with. He could have said, "Peter, I need you to watch over my people with a sturdy authority, kind of like a shepherd's staff. Make sure to lead them by still waters, guide them to grazing fields and make sure they stick together. Before you take them somewhere new, make sure there aren't any poisonous plants in the field; oh, and make sure to drive out all kinds of wolves, lions, and bears who might be hungry for lamb chops. If they're sick, bind them up. If they've got flies, anoint their heads. If they run away, spend time with them, so they remember your voice, and more importantly our Father's voice. Raise up the next generation of leaders and teach them to do the things I taught you so that you can take care of more and more sons and daughters. Remember where to lead My people after the storms of life; to the places where they can rest in the calm and be restored from the lessons of yesterday. Have you got all that Peter?"

He didn't have to say any of that. Yet He did. He essentially said, "Lead My sheep."

CHAPTER TEN

EYE OF A SEEKER

THE OPEN

There's a huge difference between looking at something and seeing something. If I'm only fixing my eyes on what I want to look at, I may end up missing what I need to see. Take tennis, for instance. I had the amazing opportunity to coach tennis for a number of years. While on the court, if I only look at the ball I may end up missing what kind of spin it was hit with. But if I see the way my opponent sets up for the shot, where he's positioned in the court and what type of swing he uses (all while looking at the ball) I can have a better guess of where that ball is going and how to approach this next shot.

Coaching taught me so much about eye contact. I already briefly explained it but let's take a deeper look. While coaching I had to make sure to make contact with the tennis ball either in a feeding style (me with a basket hitting ball after ball to my client) or in a live ball situation (where we would hit back and forth) all the while keeping my eyes on my client in order to refine their particular skill. I may be looking at the tennis ball coming toward me, but I'm also paying attention to the footwork of "Bryan" across the court. As I make contact with the ball, if Bryan hasn't hit his split step, he may not be prepared to return my shot. As I hit, I'm watching to see if he split steps. He needs to approach the ball, load his hips and hands, step in, finish the shot and recover. I'd reply in kind. As I would make moves and adjustments, Bryan was to make moves and adjustments.

Tennis is one of the most beautiful sports to watch, especially at the elite level. It is a game of two people flowing in the moment; taking charge of what they're given in order to challenge and press their opponent. Tennis is fluid and rigid. Responsive and reactive. Poise and agitation. Regal and raw. To anyone just looking at the ball, you'll miss the articulate dance of each player moving in the ever-changing tempo of the metronome on the court.

THE WIDE OPEN

Another place where fluidity meets rigid rules of force is out in the ocean. I grew up with a bodyboard beneath me and a pair of fins on my feet; whether on the sun-kissed dawn or in turbulent hurricane seas. The rush of discovering a wave, working with its raw power and accepting its energy as your own—pure adrenaline. One of the best feelings in the world is when you're getting "pitted" (as said by our surfer friend from the Internet). The wave encompasses you in this sweet pocket where air and water combine for the briefest of moments, and if you work with the wave, you'll slip out of the tube and move on, or get sucked into the torrent of its vicious undertow. Now before too many people get upset, Virginia Beach wasn't exactly the surf capital of the world; but when hurricane season came, it was a completely different shore.

There's my childhood—waves and tennis balls. They are two completely different sports with two completely different flows. But God was in the middle of it all, teaching me to see what shouldn't be seen so that I could learn to work with what I was looking at. This is how I learned to flow with Him when it came to ministry. Worship is so much like a set on the ocean. We see the waves coming, and we have the choice to pursue or pass it up for the next. Sometimes you'll choose a "wave," and it'll close out on you while other times we'll find one ripe to shred.

Pastoral ministry is so much like tennis; well, coaching tennis that is. Sometimes we're meant to stand across from one another on a court and learn how to work with each other; but then there are those times when the "coach" needs to step across the net and walk life out with the "player." How I coached was more of a play mentality instead of a win/loss mentality. We learned how to have fun in the midst of learning, not just developing skills to win or lose; because when it's only about winning and losing, we will lose everything when we don't win. That's a tough burden to carry when tennis is made up of point after point after point. If I lose one point, how can I come back to win the next point? I have to stop having a losing mentality and recognize that we're playing. I just have to keep playing and try to outplay you. There are times when you outplay me, and that's part of the game.

I've got to say this: failure is a part of the Kingdom. "For a righteous man falls seven times, and rises again," Proverbs 24:16. The Christian life isn't filled with a solid 'W' on the scorecard. It's filled with wins and losses. I invite you to step into the Kingdom of God where He made you perfectly imperfect! Where He wants to use our loses to help us play better the next time. God is not ashamed of our shortcomings, He actually may have included them in the manual for our life so that we can have eyes to see people just like us; so that our story would involve those who aren't perfect.

Can you see the parallels? I hope you're starting to see the need to not only look at what's going on but to see the deeper levels.

EYES OF A SEEKER

The best part of the Kingdom of God is this: it's filled with hidden gems and treasures for the sons and daughters of God to seek and to find. It's probably why Hide and Go Seek is one of my favorite games; I love to look for what's not seen, or at least not easily seen. But for those who are simply looking for answers in order to give them, they will ever live the life of a scoffer; dismissing the truths that others are trying to share because they want to be the distributors of truth (usually their perception of truth).

So many of us have longed to "arrive," meaning we are eagerly anticipating the day that we finally have all the answers, can take a seat and have people come ask us what we know. That's not my finish line, my finish line is heaven; and until we get there I hope to ever be a student of Holy Spirit, a son of God and a follower of Jesus Christ. Both of these sentiments seem a bit shallow, don't they? They're a bit shallow because one is seeking perfection while the other seems to accept less than perfect. Actually, the lie is hidden in the idea that we cannot and will not have access to the mysteries of God because "we only see in part and can only know in part."

1 Corinthians 2:10 (TPT) says, "But God now unveils these profound realities to us by the Spirit. Yes, he has revealed to us his inmost heart and deepest mysteries through the Holy Spirit, who constantly explores all things."

The Holy Spirit is exploring *all* things! Maybe I couldn't get an answer on something yesterday, but today the Holy Spirit is still exploring that question, and it's my job to continue in relationship with Him so that I can keep asking and He can keep revealing! This is the Holy Spirit's job! To reveal the mysteries of God to us! Out of the two schools of thought listed above, it may be better to remain a student instead of a professor. Though, I'm beginning to lean towards being a son who has relationship with the Father, Son, and Spirit. 1 Cor. 3:16 paraphrased says we are the temple of God! If the Lord dwells in us and we have the Spirit of God living in us, doesn't that mean we can have the mind of God? Of course, it does! And guess what? It's biblical!

After all, who can really see into a person's heart and know his hidden impulses except for that person's spirit? So, it is with God. His thoughts and secrets are only fully understood by his Spirit, the Spirit of God. For we did not receive the spirit of this world system but the Spirit of God, so that we might come to understand and experience all that grace has lavished upon us. And we articulate these realities with the words imparted to us by the Spirit and not with the words taught by human wisdom. We join together Spirit-revealed truths with Spirit-revealed words. Someone living on an entirely human level rejects the revelations of God's Spirit, for they make no sense to him. He can't understand the revelations of the Spirit because they are only discovered by the illumination of the Spirit. Those who live in the Spirit are able to evaluate all things carefully, and they are subject to the scrutiny of no one but God. For Who has ever intimately known the mind of the Lord Yahweh well enough to become his counselor? Christ has, and we possess Christ's perceptions.

1 Corinthians 2:11-16 TPT

The New American Standard Bible ends with "But we have the mind of Christ." Because we have the mind of Christ, we now have access to the fullness of God!

Now let me set a few things straight. I am not saying:

- I can give my own interpretation of scripture and then slap the God label on it in order to authenticate my own horse hockey!

- I never have to study scripture again because I can just go "straight to God!"

- I can make up my own set of truths so that I can live in my own world of right and wrong.

What I am saying is:

- I can now extend an invitation to God to read scripture with me so that I can come into the fullness of His intention for what He's spoken!

- I can now have beautiful, intimate, conversations with God in order to learn more of His heart.

- I can discover His nature and character to understand His truth better.

The eyes of the seeker are wide open to not only see the truths of God but to live them out in our daily lives! This means:

> *The Spirit of the Lord God is upon me,*
> *Because the Lord has anointed me*
> *To **bring good news to the afflicted**;*
> *He has sent me to **bind up the brokenhearted**,*
> *To proclaim liberty to captives and freedom to prisoners;*
> *To **proclaim the favorable year of the Lord***
> ***And the day of vengeance of our God**;*
> *To **comfort all who mourn**,*
> *To **grant those who mourn in Zion**,*
> ***Giving them a garland instead of ashes**,*
> ***The oil of gladness instead of mourning**,*
> ***The mantle of praise instead of a spirit of fainting**.*
> *So, **they will be called oaks of righteousness**,*
> *The planting of the Lord that He may be glorified.*
> Isaiah 61:1-3 NASB

It might be time to go all in and ask God for the full, hot off the press, truth. Remember, we have the mind of Christ!

FULLNESS

Based on scripture we have access to walk in the full truth that God has set for us. Unfortunately, we settle for lukewarm lies because they're easier to stomach and sometimes because we've only come to the Father halfhearted. When we accept the full Spirit of God, we will then, at *that* moment, have access to all of Him. If your theology hasn't yet accepted the place, power and role of the Holy Spirit it's not too late. Invite Him into your life! Invite Him into your theology! Invite Him into your family! Invite Him into your work!

How crazy would it be to invite the Holy Spirit into your workspace? Then begin to see coworkers getting saved! Projects getting approved! Growth in the business!

What about inviting Him into your family? What if your children started acting respectfully! Unity in the bedroom! Increase of wisdom in your finances!

What if we invited the Holy Spirit into our churches? Unity! Depth! Healing! Encouragement! Community connections!

The fullness of the Gospel involves the Holy Spirit! The fullness of the Gospel involves Jesus Christ! The Fullness of the Gospel involves the Father! The fullness of the Gospel involves every aspect of the Word of God (even those touchy verses that your church won't touch)!

Let's actively drop the lukewarm lies from the Gospel in order to enter in to the fullness of God.

About the Author

C.J. Kuenzli and his wife, Bethany, founded Land of the Living; a ministry dedicated to restoring generations to wholeness. Their heart is to make disciples and worship as they lead others toward the heart of the Father; so we all can experience His life-changing love. They desire to make every heart His home as they  travel the world. In 2019 they adopted boy & girl twin babies, Zion & Alleluia.

If you'd like to learn more about Land of the Living, attend a Rekindle Retreat or partner with the ministry visit:

www.RekindleRetreats.org

Land of the Living is a 501(c)3, nonprofit, ministry devoted to Restoring Generations to Wholeness. Our Rekindle Retreats are a spark for the heart, soul, and mind to connect with the Father, Son, and Holy Spirit.